Part Five

The Ammonite Seekers

by James David

Illustrated by James David

Cover Illustration by John Freeman

First Published in the United Kingdom in 2009
by Moonbeam Publishing

ISBN No. - 978 0954770457

cover - 'Nocturne - Whitby Eastside'
by John Freeman
9, Market Place, Whitby,
North Yorkshire, YO22 4DD
www.johnfreemanstudio.co.uk

Bibliographical Data Services
British Library Cataloguing-in-Publication Data
A catalogue record for this book is available
from the British Library

Printed and bound by:
The Max Design & Print Co
Chessingham Park Industrial Estate,
Common Road, Dunnington,
York YO19 5SE

AQUA CRYSTA

Part 1	***Next to No Time***
Part 2	***Deeper Than Yesterday***
Part 3	***Forever Crystal***
Part 4	***StoneSpell***
Part 5	***The Ammonite Seekers***

To my Mother,
and in memory of my Father,
for an inspiring childhood

AQUA CRYSTA

Part 5

The Ammonite Seekers

Chapter 1

A gentle, sleepy stillness cloaked the woodland. The chattering, swooping swallows that had scarred and stirred the warm air above *Old Soulsyke* throughout the hot, busy days of Summer had long gone. Autumn had quietly turned the Harvestlands into gold, and the swallows' nests of dried mud lay abandoned, clinging to the crumbling stone bones of the ancient farmstead. Indeed, their treasured fledglings were already thousands of miles away, following parents southwards to the Sun. With good fortune, next Spring would see them all back to the very same rocky nooks and crannies, and the chattering and swooping would begin all over again...as had happened down the centuries throughout the depths of time. The magic of nature.

Meanwhile, the small, hilltop woodland that held the deserted buildings aloft the vast, surrounding sea of planted spruce and larch, seemed at rest compared to the Summer. With the swallows flown and the dense buzzing of insects faded to almost nothing, there seemed to be an air of peace and tranquility about the place! Of course, there was still a dribbling babble of bird-song, but nothing like the daily uproar

of Summer! Chaffinches, thrushes, blue-tits, wrens, blackbirds and the rest still darted between the gnarled, old branches, helping themselves to the rich harvest of Autumn berries. Grey squirrels, too, were foraging for acorns, beechnuts, chestnuts and even the nuts from the one and only, and very rare, walnut tree! But, somehow, the exuberance of Summer had been left behind. The swallows had taken it with them, and left the woodland to the beckoning chill of Winter.

The golden island, of course, not only attracted the foraging wildlife of the Upper World. It also enticed harvesting parties up from the secret, subterranean realm of *Aqua Crysta.* For her inhabitants the season of *Wintumn* had already begun and the workings of another kind of magic were well underway. The magic of nature was one thing, but the magic of *Aqua Crysta* was something else...something completely different!

The magnificent magic of nature had steadily evolved on Planet Earth over millions and millions of years, all brilliantly woven into a single worldwide web of wildlife and wondrous creations...from rainbows to rhinoceroses, from butterflies to banyan trees, from crystals to crocodiles, from peacocks to piranhas and from sunsets to seashells! Yes, a truly magnificent magic, ignored and destroyed at Mankind's peril, but the magic of *Aqua Crysta* was different. Very different indeed! A magic of spells and enchantments unknown to the men of the Upper World and well beyond their understanding. A mystical magic treasured by her people and, very importantly, totally at one with the other magic, the original magic...the magic of Mother Nature.

At that very moment, a harvesting party from *Aqua Crysta* was sheltering beneath a single, fallen, mottled gold and yellow leaf from a sycamore tree. Rain was falling heavily and, together with the plummeting drips from the soaking branches of the canopy, the raindrops were battering the fragile shelter.

In fact, the noise was almost deafening as the foraging group of tiny

Aqua Crystans, led by Mayor Lepho, covered their ears and watched the tumbling drops of glistening water crash onto the forest floor all around them, exploding and shattering upon impact and sending smaller droplets in all directions.

Jamie...it was his first *Harvest Expedition*...gazed beyond the shelter of the crinkled leaf in amazement. Seeing raindrops smashing into the forest floor from this level...truly *ground level*...amid towering stalks of grass, giant fallen nuts and enormous leaves...was absolutely mind-blowing!! The size of the drops for one thing...each one as big as a football back in the world to which he used to belong! And the pitter-patter he once took for granted was now a brilliant feast for the eyes and ears, with the wild, watery explosions sending their shimmering cascades of transparent mini droplets crashing into one another in every direction!

Of course, the whole expedition had been a fantastic adventure!

And there had been *seven*, long Upper World days of it!

Plus *seven*, long, pretty scary Upper World nights!

Since arriving in *Aqua Crysta* with his sister after the tragic events of Midsummer, when *Deer Leap* and his father had magically vanished into thin air, he had become accustomed to the never-ending crystal light down in the welcoming, subterranean world. But here, back in the harsh Upper World, the unfriendly blackness of the night was now something to set his heart racing! Every sound that had shattered the inky silence had sent shivers down his spine. The creaks of wind blown trees, the crunches beneath fox and badger paws, not to mention the eerie calls of screeching owls tearing into the solid darkness. Thoughts of the seven nights curled up in pine-needle camps at the feet of skyscraper trees made him shiver again. Camps within root hollows where soaring pine trees seemed to plunge straight out of the earth and hold up the heavens! True, small crackling camp-fires had been lit each night to keep the silence and darkness at bay, but they had soon become just piles of glowing embers. Fortunately, the exertions of the days had brought easy sleep to Jamie each night. After delicious suppers and brilliant story-telling sessions around the camp-fires, he had fallen gratefully into his own deep dreamland, well away from his dark fears.

Indeed, the days had been full of hard work, gathering berries and nuts and loading them into carts. It had taken three Upper World days to journey from the entrance to the *Harvest Passage*way (near the well) across the barren Sprucelands to the beautifully rich wooded copse around *Old Soulsyke Farm.*

Hours upon hours of trudging over hills and dales of drifted pine-needles, pulling empty carts had eventually reaped rich rewards. The harvest had been magnificent! Acorns, hazelnuts, beechnuts, walnuts and chestnuts had all been rolled into great piles and loaded onto the carts ready for the return journey. Other carts were loaded with giant blackberries and much smaller wimberries, all gathered from bramble bushes and wimberry shrubs that swept around and between the ruins of the old farm buildings.

Of course, the woodland birds (like huge, terrifying pterodactyls to Jamie) were a constant nuisance, not to mention wasps (about as long as cricket bats) and squirrels (larger than grey, furry, bushy tailed double-decker buses!).

But amazingly, not one tiny Aqua Crystan forager was ever picked up in a bird's beak, stung by a wasp or trodden on by a squirrel! Although it has to be said that Jamie did have *one* particular close shave when an enormous magpie swooped out of the blue towards him! He was just gathering a superb, scrumptiously juicy, almost bursting blackberry from its bush, when he suddenly saw the

great sweeping black and white wings rushing towards him, great talons aiming for the very berry that he was gathering! In a split second he swung out of the way on the berry's thin twig, just as the talons sank into the purple flesh, showering him from head to toe with the delicious juice! A group of Aqua Crystans beneath him were also soaked in purple but they all burst into laughter as Jamie tumbled into their arms!

Under the crinkly sycamore leaf roof, the twenty two harvesters began to sing a song to keep up their strength and pass the time until the rain stopped. At least it was daylight, thought Jamie, as he watched the rain drops, and tried to join in the singing...but even better, this was the last day of the expedition. Soon he would be back with his sister in their house in Pillo!
Back in the cosiness of *Aqua Crysta*!
Not that he hadn't enjoyed the journey back into the Upper World, of course. It had been a fantastic adventure...but the thoughts of being back within the warm, comfortable enchantment of *Aqua Crysta* made him smile to himself.
"What's tickling you?" suddenly came the equally warm and comforting voice of Lepho, the ginger haired and ginger whiskered Mayor of Pillo and chief advisor to Queen Venetia.
"I bet you all the bramble wine in the *Larder Caves* that you're day-dreaming about being back down there in Pillo with your sister...and Jonathan and Jane...!"

"And Lucius and Grizelda...and Gabrielle...and Dodo...and the crystalids... and the beautiful Floss Cavern...and all that *wonderful* food!!" burst Jamie. "I just *can't wait* to get back!"
He suddenly felt a pang of guilt, and his beaming smile vanished.
"But, of course, I've had a fantastic time up here! It's been brill!"
Lepho looked at him knowingly, his bluey-eyes twinkling beneath his ginger eyebrows.

"We all feel *exactly* the same! *I* do! *They* do!" he said, glancing at the singing Aqua Crystans. "We *all* can't wait to return down there! Seven Upper World days and nights is a long, long time...full to the brim with every possible kind of peril. But it's not so much the dangers we all face that fill our minds...it's the thoughts and memories of *Aqua Crysta* that constantly enter our heads! And it's the same for everyone! One moment you're filling a cart with cut up toadstools, the next you're gazing up at the waterfalls at Pillo!! One moment you're rolling a juicy bramble berry over the forest floor, the next you're aboard the '*Goldcrest'* sailing along the Floss, ploughing through countless rafts of froth and waving up at the folk who live at Middle Floss. It's fantastic! It's the imagination. It's absolutely wonderful! But I'll let you into a little secret!"
Jamie's young eyes looked into the wisdom of Lepho's.
"It's *never ever* the other way round!" whispered the Mayor.
Jamie, under his own mass of bushy ginger hair, looked puzzled.
Lepho smiled.
"When you're down in *Aqua Crysta*," he said, "you never ever think of the Upper World in the same way! Never!"
The light-bulb of understanding suddenly switched on in Jamie's head!
"You mean like when you're at school, slaving away at maths, you're always thinking in your imagination about what you're doing after school or during the hols...but when you're having fun after school or during the school hols...you *never ever* think of how good it would be to be sitting in your classroom, at your desk, slaving away at maths!"
Lepho looked at his young friend, and winked.
"Got it in one!" he announced. "Someday, my boy, you will be a fountain of wisdom. Just listen and ...!"
Suddenly he stopped...and they both raised their eyes to the sombre, steely skies.
The singing stopped, and everyone gathered around the very edge of the leaf shelter and gazed up into the heavy, rain-filled grey that seemed to be held up by the dripping towering trees themselves.
A sound had been heard.
A strange, unfamiliar sound!

From somewhere up in the branches of the trees.
A terrifying sound!
A sound that sent shivers of fear down all twenty-two spines!
And a sound that banished from the minds of the Aqua Crystans all thoughts of returning to the comforts of home.
The sound grew louder as the skies darkened!
The weight of it all seemed to crush the tiny foragers down into the damp forest floor itself.
Hands were rammed onto ears to keep the sound at bay.
Wild, darting eyes stared panic-stricken into the gloom, trying to see its source.
What could be the origin of such haunting, horrific, ear-piercing cries?

Everyone gazed up into the gloom, dreading what would happen next!

And then...

...they saw it!!!

Chapter 2

Meanwhile, and exactly at the same time, Jessica was neither in the Upper World, nor was she in *Aqua Crysta*!
She was in Scotland!

Safe and snug within the warm, cosy arms of '*Ben More*'...the wooden chalet on the edge of the *Queen Mary Plantation* which cloaked the toes of the mountain that shared its name with the homely log cabin.
Ruth, her mother, busy darning socks, sunk deeply in her armchair by the roaring fire in the living room, her long, coppery hair cascading over an embroidered cushion.

Jessica, just five years old, was sitting at her feet, feeling the glowing warmth from the fire on her cheeks and reading the words in her favourite picture book and gazing at the detailed illustrations.
The book...'*Scotland in the Wild*' was her greatest treasure.
It had been one of her Christmas presents from a couple of years before, just after the Dawson family had moved into *Ben More*. The wooden house had come with her dad's new job as Plantation Manager.
That first Christmas was brilliant. So magical. It had snowed and

snowed, and the very young Jessica and her even younger brother Jamie had had a wonderful time. But it was the Spring afterwards when Jessica had fallen in love with the natural beauty that surrounded the log cabin. The mountains and waterfalls, the winding forest paths and shady glades had captivated her, as too had the wild animals...the red deer, the polecats, the squirrels, the foxes and badgers and hedgehogs...

And here they all were in her treasured picture book, in startling detail, with almost every single hair of their fur drawn by the artist and set in the most wonderful woodland scenery, so rich and deep.

She would stroke the animals with a finger tip and wish she could walk into the pictures themselves, along the fern edged paths.

Best of all was the middle of the book with one great picture spreading over the two huge pages, with every possible creature hidden somewhere within the beautiful forest scene, their names printed by each one.

Indeed, the names of the animals and birds were the first words she had learned to read, with the help of her mother.

Jessica, looked into the flames of the fire and imagined herself out in the forest at her favourite place...a quiet, sun dappled dell, with a miniature babbling brook rushing over mossy, crystal rocks. She was just about to feed a handful of peanuts to 'Squiggs', a red squirrel she had befriended, when suddenly she heard a voice ringing in her ears.

"Jessica, Jessica, wake up! You're going to be late!"

Her eyes opened dozily, one after the other, and she squinted in the pinkish light. She felt a hand nudge her arm.

"Wh...where am I?" she mumbled.

Gone had the book and the flames of the fire.

Gone had the cosy rug and the snug armchair.

And the voice certainly wasn't her mother's!

"You're in your house in Pillo!"

Jessica looked into the face that hovered above her. It was beaming the widest smile you could imagine. It was Jane, her dark plaits bobbing in the scented air.

"You've been fast asleep! But you've got to get up and get your skates on! Remember, you're the 'Guest of Honour' and everyone's already crowding into the *Meeting Hall Cavern*! Rudolph and Guinevere are ready to take us!"

Jessica rubbed her eyes and sat up.

"I must have been dreaming!" she whispered. "I was miles and miles away...in our log cabin in Scotland! I must only have been about five or six years old..."

She slowly gazed around the room that she had shared with her brother since they'd arrived in *Aqua Crysta* back in the Upper World Summer.

It was difficult to think that *this* was reality!

Being *here* was more like being in a dream!

It seemed as though she'd woken up and stepped into her own dream-world!

And it had been exactly the same, every time she'd fallen asleep, since the moment she and her brother had been given the tiny house in Pillo...next door to Jonathan and Jane.

There was just the one room...or rather, cave...but wow! What a room it was! Her single bed was at the back of the hollow that had been carved out of the same white and pink crystal rock that made up most of *Aqua Crysta*. The walls were uneven with all sorts of nooks and crannies, and shelves and alcoves, all packed with carved crystal ornaments and piles of unworked raw crystals. And, of course, the rosy-pink glow that softly shone from every single crystal face filled the hollow with a constant, warm light, just like the rest of the magical world.

Indeed, there was no difference between the glow within the room and that which illuminated the whole of the Floss Cavern. The light was eternal and always of the same brightness. It never suddenly glowed stronger nor faded. There was no switching it on and off, and, because the light came from every surface, there were no shadows!

At the foot of her bed was a towering dandelion clock, its seeds perfectly in place to form a softly shining sphere almost as

wide as her bed. She often imagined blowing it to tell the time and watching the delicate seeds floating around the room...but she'd never dared! After all, she thought, it would ruin forever the perfect natural beauty of the great globe! It could never be put together again...and besides, it would take dozens and dozens of blows to dislodge all the seeds!! It would be at least ninety-nine o'clock before she'd finished!
Scattered about the smooth crystal floor were several green, curly oak-leaves acting as a sort of carpet. Each one looked as fresh as the day it had been picked, all glossy and bright. Of course, nothing ever decayed in the world of *Aqua Crysta*! By them was a single acorn, still in its rough brown cup. Jamie had already carved great chunks out of the nut and toasted many thin slices. They were absolutely delicious, especially if smothered with bramble jelly or piled up with toadstool cream and toasted heather tips!
Towards the door was another carpet, this time woven from dyed grasses from the *Harvestlands*. It was mainly purple, maroon and mauve with a huge golden '*AC'* across its middle. There was a smaller mat of the same design by the door, this time with a golden '*Pillo*' delicately woven across.
Next to the carpet was a wonderfully carved wooden table with swirling grain patterns turning and twisting so much that they almost brought its surface to life. Matching shelves and chairs surrounded it, but it was an amazing knot-hole in the table-top that delighted Jessica the most!

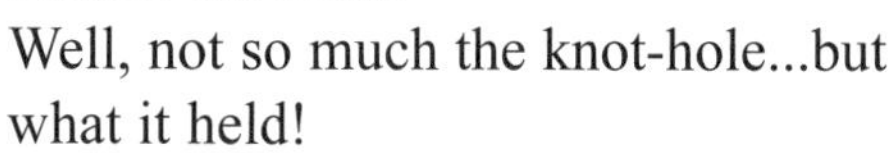

Well, not so much the knot-hole...but what it held!
For sweeping up from the floor, through the hole and into the miniature forest of little stalactites that clung to the ceiling...was a feather... a jay feather...a black and white feather, shot through with brilliant, iridescent blues! The good luck charm of *Aqua Crysta*! The most prized possession of any household. Jessica often sat at the table and just stared at it, letting its beauty and significance soak into her being. It was

stunning to look at closely, with its countless intricate strands of feathery softness, all flowing from the slender, curved, tapering, hollow, creamy white stalk.

Even as she pulled on her heather coloured Aqua Crystan smock, fastened her belt and slid her feet into her snug, beaten bark sandals, she looked into its sheen, captivated by its power.

"A feather is somehow the solution to the mystery! Definitely!" she said with determination, as Jane leaned on the lower half of the door gazing across to the Pillo Falls.

"I suppose you're talking about the secret code in the ammonites!" she called. "But how can a feather have anything to do with it?"

"I don't know for sure," said Jessica, lightly stroking the quill, and looking up to the ceiling, "but I can feel it in my bones. Something is going to happen up there in the *Harvestlands* and all I can say is that it involves a feather to match Chandar, the albino roe deer!"

"You mean a *white* feather?"

Jessica nodded.

"Yes, a pure white feather, as dazzlingly white as fresh, driven snow!"

"But, there are *no* birds of the forest with pure white feathers!" insisted Jane, opening the door.

"Then the bird will be a strange visitor, one that is perhaps lost or has been blown off course by the wind!" whispered Jessica. "But it will somehow give us the clue we need to solve the fossils' code!"

Indeed, the two golden ammonites, which Jessica and Jamie had found during the Summer amid the desolate foundations of the vanished *Deer Leap* cottage, had proved to be an unsolvable mystery. All the wise and good of *Aqua Crysta* had failed to come up with their meaning. Mayor Lepho, Lucius the Alchemist, Quentin and Toby (the elders who guarded *Lumina*, the eternal candle flame), the wise and ancient crystal carver, George Chubb...even Her Majesty, Queen Venetia herself...they had all failed to crack the mysterious code, carved into the golden spirals.

A generous reward had even been offered!

Anyone who could solve the ammonite mystery would not only be 'Guest of Honour' at the opening of the new spectacular extravaganza

in the *Meeting Hall Cavern*, but would also receive a lifetime's free supply of food and drink from the *Larder Caves*!!
(You can therefore probably guess that Jamie had been busy trying to crack the code almost non-stop since he arrived in *Aqua Crysta*...but with no success, much to his annoyance!)
The ammonites themselves now stood on a crystal plinth at the entrance to the *Meeting Hall Cavern* for any budding detective or genius to inspect. But so far, the rewards had remained unclaimed.
Of course, Jessica and Jamie knew in their hearts of hearts that the secret message that lay within the spirals would lead them to their father who had vanished along with *Deer Leap*. They were sure that, one day, they would be re-united with their dad *and* their woodland cottage! For the moment they were certain that Mr Dawson and *Deer Leap* were lost in the magic of that fateful Midsummer Night, when the sorceries of Good and Bad had locked horns at Stonehenge. On that occasion, Good had triumphed over Bad, but the trouble was...the magic that had taken Mr Dawson and *Deer Leap* was *Shym-ryn* magic!
Not Good magic, but magic of the very worst kind, especially when seasoned with revenge!
The code just had to be cracked!!

Jessica cast a final glance at the jay feather, closed the door and made her way to the edge of the rocky balcony which looked over the Floss towards the Falls. And there, patiently waiting below, was a pair of beautifully coloured crystalids hovering in mid-air ready to carry their young mistresses to the spectacle which was about to open in the *Meeting Hall Cavern.*

The girls climbed aboard Rudolph and Guinevere, gripped the creatures' necks with their knees and clung onto the antennae of the gorgeous, glassy, rainbow creatures.

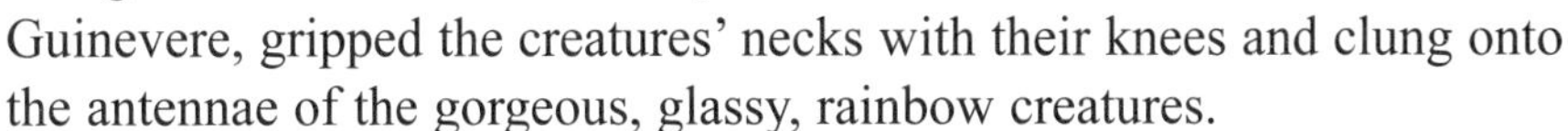

The journey ahead would be short and magical itself, but Jessica had other things on her mind...her father, *Deer Leap*, the

ammonite code...and what *was* her brother up to at that very moment in the perilous Upper World?
Was he safe?
Yes, Lepho would see to that!
She just wished that he was back home, climbing aboard his crystalid called Sabre so they could fly down the Floss together...but he *had* so desperately *wanted* to experience being part of a foraging party, and being only a couple of inches tall in the Upper World!
He'd almost begged her to let him go, and in the end she'd gone against her better judgement and allowed him to accompany the group.
Boys will be *boys*, she'd reckoned!
And, after all, he *would* be constantly under the eagle eye of Lepho!
Yes, he'd definitely return safe and sound! There was nothing at all to worry about! She was certain! In no time, he'd be sitting at the wooden table tucking into a toasted slice of acorn and probably full to the brim of terrifying tales about near-misses under the hooves of stampeding deer and being chased by Aqua Crystan eating spiders!
She would never hear the end of it!!

But if she'd known what was just about to happen to Jamie up there in the Forest, her blood would have run ice-cold!
For the danger he was in...was absolutely immense!
And could well mean that Jessica would *never ever* see her brother *again*!!
Death was just around the corner!
And about to slither and slide from a dark, damp hiding place!

Chapter 3

From their crinkly leaf shelter near the foot of a gigantic sycamore tree, the startled and puzzled Aqua Crystans gazed up among the bare branches that fractured the grey sky. At first they couldn't make anything out at all, just a blur of criss-crossed boughs. The distance from the roots to the treetop was too far to focus properly, never mind the exploding raindrops hindering their vision. But gradually, they made out a single, giant, white, moving shape...a giant, bright white bird, perched on a branch and flapping its snowy wings erratically to balance itself. The bird, the like of which no Aqua Crystan had ever seen, was the source of the terrifying cry...or rather, screech!

"In all my Harvest visits to the Upper World, I have never witnessed such a bird!" whispered Lepho. "Our flying friends of the Forest are generally much, much smaller and certainly not dazzling white in plumage! Even our larger jays and magpies are nowhere near the size of this noisy stranger, nor are our black rooks and crows!"

The harsh, raucous cry of the bird seemed to be never ending as it threw back its large white head and screamed its songless screech into the damp air, over and over again!
The watching Aqua Crystans' fear was slowly replaced by curiosity as, one by one, they risked the falling raindrops, stepped gingerly from their cover and gazed upwards at the strange source of the din.
"I think I know what it is!" announced Jamie, with a smile crossing his face at last.
Lepho and the others lowered their gaze and looked at him.
"It's a gull! A seagull!" he beamed. "From the coast! Probably from the cliffs near Whitby! They catch fish and such like from the sea! It could be a herring gull, or a black-backed gull...or a kittiwake...or a fulmar!"
He was beginning to sound like a real expert and his beaming smile grew wider and wider! He was revelling in the fact that *he*, for a change, was *actually* telling the wise old Lepho something...instead of the other way round!
Smiles even broke across the faces of all the other foragers!
Even the rain stopped!
The Aqua Crystans ventured further from their shelter and gazed into the brightening skies.

Suddenly, a smaller, jet black rook appeared and perched near the white gull. It began to reply to the gull's scream with its own tuneless call, "*Kraak*! *Kraak*! *Kraak*!" 
Then another appeared, then another!
Soon there must have been thirty or more, all croaking in unison!
It seemed that a whole rookery had arrived to inspect the stranger, clothing the bare sycamore tree in sombre black! The din was almost deafening, and the Aqua Crystans once again covered their ears. And in the midst of all the deathly black was the solitary, snow white gull, still throwing its head back, screeching its message and taking not the slightest bit of notice of the crowd it had attracted!

However...way below, unknown to any of the emboldened harvesters and not too far away from them...the treetop din

had aroused a new danger! The uproarious hubbub was so great that it had even awakened the sleeping deaf!
The raucous sound had vibrated through the forest air so much that its echoes had even crept beneath a roughly strewn pile of stones on the forest floor...and into a damp, hidden cavity.
A deadly cavity that played winter host to a tangled knot of poison!
The lair of a dozen or more hibernating snakes.
Adders!
Venomous adders!
Their bite lethal to small mammals and certainly to Aqua Crystans!
The sound vibrations fingered their scales and, slowly but surely, each serpent cast sleep aside and regained an unwelcome consciousness.
They had expected to hibernate during the dark months, allowing their chill blood to become even colder. But the tangled knot had to respond to the sudden alarm. The snakes could be under threat from some unknown beast of the forest. They had to act as one single deadly creature! Rapid movement was out of the question...they needed the warmth of the Sun to heat their blood...but there was *no* Sun! Without it they would remain torpid, sluggish...and vulnerable.
Lidless eyes began to stare unblinkingly into the damp, soily darkness.
Somehow, Mother Nature was making her most despised offspring stir into action.
The tangled knot began to writhe as though the friction created by grinding scales warmed the blood of the individual serpents. 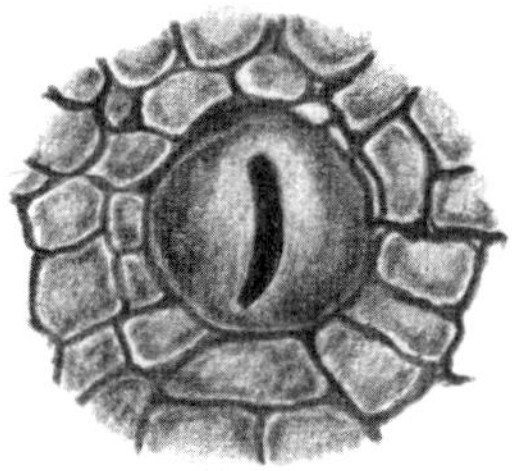
Forked tongues began to dart in and out sensing the air.
They sensed another kind of warmth.
The warmth of prey!
An unexpected winter feast!
Aqua Crystans!
The tangled knot began to unravel.
The lethal head of the first adder glided menacingly from the dark cavity and out from under the concealing stones. In a moment its staring eyes spotted the feast. All thoughts of the threat from the uproar in the

treetops vanished. All thoughts were now fixed on the twenty-two tiny, warm blooded mouthfuls that lay just a single snake's length away!
A feast indeed!!

As the pair of beautiful crystalids silently swooped down from the Upper Terraces of Pillo and glided serenely over the town, Jessica, gazed into the shimmering Floss, way below.
And what a sight it was! A never-ending, flowing, gleaming ribbon of pink, buffeted in an imaginary breeze, weaving this way and that along the wonderful, winding, crystal cavern.
During her time down in the magical realm living next door to Jonathan and Jane in Pillo, it was her journeys throughout the kingdom, clinging onto Rudolph, her copper hair streaming behind, that had given her the most pleasure. The exhilarating, breath-taking flights had even eased the pain of losing her father and *Deer Leap*. They were a sort of antidote to the sorrow she mostly felt. A kind of release from the heartache.

Suddenly, as though the crystalids understood and could read her mind perfectly, they soared high above the river.
Higher and higher, almost up into the forest of plunging stalactites that clung from the cavern's ceiling.
Jessica gazed downwards in stunned amazement.
Never had she flown this high!
The view was incredible!
The ribbon of pink seemed to shrink as the towering heights of both cavern walls could be seen at once. It reminded her of the very first time she and her brother had jumped down from the bottom of the well.
The time they'd jumped through the magical mists...and, in a split second, they'd landed on the shore of what, a moment before, had been a mere trickle, just inches wide...but had, in an instant, become the great winding River Floss.
"Look!" called Jane from Guinevere. "Can you make out all the boats heading for the *Meeting Hall Cavern*? We'll be there before any of them!"
Jessica didn't reply.
She was totally lost in her daydream...although she had to keep

reminding herself that this was for real, not a teasing happening in her sleep, like her visit to *Ben More* log cabin!
She was enjoying every single thing that flooded into her eyes.
Her thirst for the pictures was almost unquenchable.
She just wished the feast could be never-ending, but she knew that the journey would soon be over.
The myriads of glittering, ever twinkling crystals, the soaring, precipitous pinky-white walls, the slender stalactites...

But just then...very strangely...a giant image...no, two giant images...began to form below her, in the midst of the cavern, hovering between the walls and above the ribbon of the river.
Two great, transparent faces began to appear in the great void!
Faces she knew well and loved with all her heart.
One was the smiling, freckly face of her brother, crowned with a tangled fringe of ginger hair...the other was the black-bearded, blue-eyed face of her father. He looked grim and unhappy, dried bloody wounds ripping across his cheeks, purply bruises blushing angrily around his eyes.
Jessica's eyes were both entranced and frightened by the images...
...but then, to her horror, she noticed through the faces, the winding River Floss...way, way below...had turned from a delicate, pink ribbon into a writhing, scaly serpent!
A brownish, tarnished gold snake, its fearsome length scarred from end to end with a harsh, dark, jagged zig-zag.
Suddenly, its head with staring, unblinking eyes and spitting, forked tongue seemed to soar upwards towards the hovering images.
Its great mouth opened wider and wider!
Two glinting white fangs were unsheathed from the upper jaw, both dripping with yellow venom...!
Jessica let out an anguished scream of terror as the serpent's poisonous head climbed ever upwards towards the images of the familiar faces.
"They're going to be bitten! They're going to die!" she yelled at the top of her voice, her words bouncing and echoing between the cavern walls.
And then, in her panic...her grasp of Rudolph's antennae suddenly loosened, and she felt herself slide down her steed's smooth, glassy neck!

Her arms wildly flailed in the warm air, her hands tried to grab at what they could...but it was all in vain...

...and as the ferocious, gleaming, deadly fangs reached their prey...she plunged head over heels into the same vast images that had been conjured from nothing.

She would at last be re-united with her beloved father and brother...

...but the coming together...

...would be *in death*!!!

Chapter 4

It was Lepho who noticed it first. The great serpent's poisonous head sliding over the crinkled leaves of the forest floor towards his defenceless compatriots.

"*NADER*! *NADER*!" he screamed against the deafening din from the treetops.

"*NADER*! *NADER*!" he called again, sweeping Jamie off his feet and running for one of the giant root hollows at the base of the sycamore. He knew more than anybody that the nader was the deadliest of all the creatures of the Harvestlands. He also knew that survival would be almost impossible if a hibernating horde of snakes had been disturbed!

Jamie glanced back over his shoulder and gazed in horror at the blood-curdling scene behind him.

Already the giant, slithering serpent had caught up with one fleeing Aqua Crystan who was struggling to run over the leaves.

Eldred didn't stand a chance! In one terrifying moment, the serpent's cavernous mouth gaped open, the sabre fangs were drawn downwards,

and with an anguished scream the helpless Aqua Crystan was impaled through the middle by one of the venomous weapons. He struggled in vain as the gigantic dagger hinged inwards and the adder closed its jaws! Poor Eldred had been captured, killed and swallowed in little more than a handful of terrifying, agonizing moments!
Jamie felt distraught and helpless.
There was nothing anyone could have done!
The creatures knew no mercy.
Another adder appeared out of the gloom and then another, all chasing the scurrying, panic-stricken Aqua Crystans.
From a nookish cranny in the sycamore's bark, Jamie, his heart pounding, peeped out from behind Lepho's heather coloured cloak and witnessed two more of his friends captured and killed in the mere blink of an eye...Spencer and Guy.
The carnage was like nothing he had ever seen.
He felt despair mixed with his fear.
Would he and Lepho be next?
He soon had his answer!
Yet another adder's darting forked tongue had sensed the warmth of bodies at the foot of the tree!
Both Lepho and Jamie spotted it together.
The great scaly, brown head was on its way towards its prey!
Jamie was numb with fear.
The sight before him was awesome!
The staring, determined, disc-like, golden eyes each split down the middle by thin, vertical, black-slit pupils...enclosed by gleaming armour plate... and following the commanding, must-be-obeyed, fearsome, quivering tongue.
Closer and closer...
Closer and closer...

Jessica plunged through the warm, scented air towards the giant, hovering, transparent images that had been conjured below her.
Closer and closer!
Closer and closer!

The vast faces seemed to swell in size!
She was almost there!
She couldn't stop!
"Jamie! Dad! Watch out! It's behind you!" she called out, her copper hair streaming behind her.
A split second later, she was tumbling *into* Jamie's face!
She was actually *inside* the image!
It had no substance at all!
It was just made of air.
On and on she fell, next towards the snake which was thrusting upwards to meet her, its jaws agape, its gleaming fangs still dripping with venom!
She could see clearly the inside of the enormous mouth and the beginnings of the tunnel like throat...
Closer and closer!
Closer and closer...
...and then, in a trice, the serpentine image was gone.
Vanished into thin air!

And so did the one at the foot of the sycamore tree!
At the very same moment!
Just inches away from its prey, it was suddenly swept backwards as though something had got hold of its tail and jerked it upwards and away!

Lepho and Jamie watched in total amazement as the creature flew through the air cloaked in a spiralling cloak of purple mist!
Then another snake flew backwards into the air, then another!
Each shrouded in the same purple mist!
Soon, all had been dispatched, sent well away into the forest.
For the moment the survivors of the attack were safe and breathed sighs of relief, all deeply sorrowful for their lost friends.

Lepho and Jamie crept from their nookish cranny.
The young traveller looked puzzled.
He had recognised the swirling haze that enveloped the snakes and had felt the same chill in the air he had felt before...during the Summer.
"It's the *Shym-ryn*, Lepho!" he whispered at last. "It's the *Shym-ryn*! But *why* have they *saved* us?"

And at the very same instant as he uttered the word '*Shym-ryn*' in the Upper World, the hand of fate saved Jessica!
She was still tumbling through the air towards the Floss, which was becoming wider and wider as *she* rushed towards *it*, and *it* rushed towards *her*!
Air whooshed past her ears!
Her head was spinning!
The cavern walls were spinning!
She tried to scream, but nothing came out!
More air just rushed in!
Faster and faster!
She shut her eyes and gritted her teeth!
Death was surely close!
Nothing could stop it!
Closer and closer!
Closer and closer...
and then, miraculously, a hand grabbed hers and swept her up into the air!
She had been saved!
Death had been but seconds away!
She opened her eyes...and there was the beautiful sight of Guinevere the crystalid and Jane's outstretched hand and her beaming face!
"We've done it! At last, we've done it!" called Jane against the noise of the flowing Floss. "We've been weaving in and out all the way down trying to catch you...and Rudolph, of course!"
Just behind Guinevere, the other crystalid glided, as calmly and graciously as usual, but with a guilty look on its rainbow face.
"It wasn't *your* fault, Rudi!!" Jessica called breathlessly, still grasping Jane's hand, "But please come over here, and let me get back on you!"

Both crystalids came to a steady hover, and a very relieved rider climbed aboard Rudolph.
"But how did you fall off?" asked Jane. "We were having a super journey!"
"I'll try and explain when we reach the *Meeting Hall Cavern*!" replied Jessica. "But I certainly owe you a huge 'thankyou'!"
"It was nothing really!" laughed Jane. "I always knew we'd catch you, but I must say we left it to the last possible moment! It was great fun! Spiralling downwards trying to grab hold of you was like being on a gigantic invisible helter-skelter! It was brill!"
"Talking of invisibility, did you see, er...any great big images of faces in the air?" wondered Jessica hesitantly.
Jane shook her head.
"Not even a snake?" asked Jessica.
"I certainly didn't! Yuk!! You wouldn't have seen me for dust if there'd been a snake around!!"
Jessica laughed, and with that the two girls headed onwards to their destination, hoping that the rest of the journey would be completely uneventful! But as the pair of crystalids glided effortlessly above the Floss, Jessica couldn't help thinking about her brother and her father. She was convinced that they were both in danger.
The images of their faces had seemed so real!
And so had the snake!
But she knew that she was helpless.
There was nothing she could do.

As Rudolph and Guinevere swooped down towards the colourful and welcoming sight of the vast entrance of the *Meeting Hall Cavern*, she just hoped and prayed that everything would turn out well in the end... and that sometime soon they'd all be together again!
The crystalids slowed to a gentle hover, just above the excited Aqua Crystans as the winding queues slowly shuffled their way into the Hall from all the bobbing boats moored by the long quay.
Jessica smiled and waved, and looked as happy as she could.
But behind the smile was an anxious and disturbed girl.
And she had every right to be so!

If she had known what was to come...what perils lay ahead...what sights she would witness and horrors she would endure... she would have flown straight back to Pillo at that very moment, buried herself under her bedsheets and lost herself in her dreams of *Ben More*!!
But the easy way was not an option.
Instead, she was on the edge of falling into the most dangerous and terrifying venture so far...

...and, it was all just about to begin!

Chapter 5

Meanwhile, up in the *Harvestlands*, as the injured were being tended and the survivors kept a nervous look-out for more adders, a strange but understandable gloom had settled on the foragers.
Gone had the singing and happy thoughts of home.
Instead, the sudden attack and the deaths of friends and compatriots had shocked everyone to the core. The normal loving hands of Mother Nature had somehow, for the first time in Aqua Crystan history, let them down. Never before had a single life been lost during an Upper World foraging expedition. Never! But after Lepho's sad duty of counting his remaining comrades had been completed, he solemnly announced that *seven* were missing...all presumed dead. It had, indeed, been a dark, dark day in the Upper World. The worst he had known in his whole life.
He gathered the party together to announce his plan for returning to the homeland.
But before he began, he pointed into the tree-tops.
The rooks were still there, but the solitary white visitor had vanished. As, too, had the raucous din that had shaken the forest and awakened the venomous reptiles. Now there was just an eerie silence without a single trace of birdsong. All that could be heard was the dripping of water, as drip after drip fell onto the crinkled leaves and gently echoed across the golden floor.

Lepho looked at the dismal faces of his country-men.
"Never before have I known such a tragedy!" he began in a tone unknown to any of his listeners. "I have not the words to express my sorrow and regret..."
"None of it is *your* fault!" came an angry cry from the back of the gathered men. "It's *them*! Them *black spirits of death*!"
Everyone, including Jamie, gazed once more into the tree-tops.
The black cloak was still silently strewn across the branches.
There must have been a hundred or more birds, all noiselessly preening their feathers in a uninterested, couldn't-care-less sort of way.
"You may be right, Clement! You may be right! But for now, we must think of what we do next!" said Lepho, in an attempt to divert his men back to his plan for returning to *Aqua Crysta.*
"There is still danger lurking out there. The naders that magically withdrew their attack will, if they survived their unexpected flights, be on their way back to their winter lair. We must leave now and make haste for the *Harvest Passageway*!"
"And just abandon our hard-gained harvest!" came another voice. "That's what we ventured here for! That's what those seven dead souls gave their lives for!"
"The journey back home will be slow and perilous if we have to haul the loaded carts!" insisted Lepho. "We must make h...!"
Suddenly, he stopped and looked up into the grey gloom.
The eyes of the foragers also gazed up into the branches.
What they saw made them gasp!
For beyond the black, feathery shroud that was draped across the woody canopy a cloud had appeared.
A glistening white cloud, brilliant against the dull, sombre grey.
But the cloud was no ordinary one. One full of innocent mists and watery vapours.
It was a cloud with a purpose.
It was a cloud moulded from a flock of birds...snowy white seabirds...drifted in from the Whitby coast.
The single gull seen earlier must have been a spy, a scout...one sent in to judge the lie of the land.

It had returned with an army!
There must have been a thousand, all hovering and treading the damp air above the black rooks of the forest. White outnumbered black by at least ten to one!
What happened next, way above the tiny Aqua Crystan spectators, happened quickly and decisively.
The throb of beating white wings began to pulsate louder and louder through the air.
The cloud was descending into the tree-tops.
The rooks had already stopped preening and began to look concerned.
Then, all at once, as if ordered by a hidden General, the screeching of the sea-birds started in unison. The din grew louder and louder!
Several shaky '*kraaks*' tried to take on the concerted shriek of the sea-birds, but to no avail.
The battle was lost before it had begun.
With a great flutter of black, the cloak of rooks took to the air.
True, there were one or two skirmishes between black and white, but within seconds the glistening, white cloud had serenely displaced the gloomy shroud of blackness and the trees were dressed in an unexpected foliage of snow!
Then the screeching ceased as abruptly as it had started.
Silence fell upon the trees and the astonished observers on the forest floor.
Jamie wondered what on earth was going to happen next.
He hadn't long to wait.
As he gazed up into the dazzling brightness, he caught sight of one...two...three...four...five pure white feathers floating downwards from the tree-tops.
More and more began to fall, all gracefully tumbling from the cloud and all dancing and swaying from side to side as they slowly drifted and spun to the ground as if held aloft on invisible threads.
A new pitter-patter began as the first ones gently touched down upon the golden carpet...each one as long as at least half a dozen Aqua Crystans linked head to toe!
They were enormous...but so light!

More and more fell from the skies until the crinkly gold beneath the trees had all but vanished.
It was then that a strange magic began. One that had never been witnessed before, even by Lepho. Never once had he read about it in his voluminous library, nor had he heard of it in the countless tales he'd listened to by countless camp-fires!
This was something new.

Firstly, as the tumble of feathers slowed and then stopped altogether, the snowy plumes on the ground began to twitch and fidget as though tweaked by unseen fingers. There was no hint of breeze or draught or anything else that could have moved them.
Then, to the amazement of the foragers, the feathers began to form themselves into shapes...shapes that reminded the Aqua Crystans of the stream-lined hulls of ships or galleons, like the '*Goldcrest*'!
Within a minute, the veiled and hidden fingers had fashioned eight such vessels, each one formed from a dozen feathers.
The foraging party looked at one another with astonishment.
"The magic is with us!" whispered Lepho to Jamie and the others. "From whence it comes I do not know, but the picture is clear to me. We have to take advantage of it! Men, load the harvest into the bows!"

As quickly as they could possibly work, the brambles, wimberries, heather tips, fern fronds, acorns, walnuts, sycamore keys, toadstools, birch bark and mosses were loaded into the elegant, feathery sail-less boats until each was brimful with cargo.
Two Aqua Crystans manned each vessel and stood at the pointed prows, harvest piled behind them. Lepho and Jamie stood side by side at the prow of the boat full of wimberries.
"Now what's going to happen?" asked Jamie as he looked at the fleet of feathered ships like some strange armada ready to set sail.
"If my hunch is corr...!" replied Lepho.
His voice fell silent and he grabbed hold of his young charge.
Together, they felt their boat lifting into the air.
It hovered, slightly swaying on invisible waves.
Jamie looked to his side.
All the ships were floating off the ground, ready for a magical voyage.

He could feel his heart beating faster and faster!
Question after question buzzed through his mind!
What magic was at work?
Who or what was behind it?
Where would the boats take them?
Why was it all happening?
Suddenly, all his queries vanished.
The journey had begun!

Slowly but surely, the soft bundles of woven feathers began to glide smoothly forwards over the forest floor.
The magical fleet had set forth without a single mast nor sail to be seen!
Jamie stared downwards as his boat picked up speed and the rushing breeze tousled his ginger hair. Within moments the snowy white was left behind and the golds and yellows and oranges and reds flew by beneath the hull in a constant, dizzy blur.
He glanced behind to see the rest of the ships following, winding effortlessly between the trees!
What *was* the magic that was guiding the tillerless fleet...
...and to which distant harbour were they heading?

Wisps of purple mist breathed from the stern of each boat gave the answer to one of the questions, but they were unseen by the excited and awe-struck crews. As the wisps dissolved in the wakes of the speeding vessels, a cold, haunting laughter could be heard in the distant depths of the forest.
The *Shym-ryn* were out and about!
And their wicked scheme was running as smoothly as the feathered boats over the forest floor.
This time, it was *their* magic that would win!
This time, the Bad Magic would vanquish the Good.
And revenge would be sweet!!
Very sweet indeed!!

Chapter 6

The grand entrance to the *Meeting Hall Cavern* was sparkling like it had never done before. The great arch that edged the yawning mouth had been studded with hundreds of new, particularly bright and vivid white and pink crystals. All the Aqua Crystans, as they shuffled from the Floss quays into the enormous cavern, stared open-mouthed at the wonderful, luminous splendour above them.

It was quite magnificent and certainly added to the growing excitement of the expectant 'first night' audience.

As the crowds patiently moved into the vast amphitheatre, the excited talk was all about Dillip Penlop's new theatrical work. It was said to be his best ever and for several harvests there had been much anticipation as to what the story-line would be. All the many actors, actresses, scenery builders and musicians had even been sworn to secrecy. The only clues that had leaked out were that the musical show was set in the *Harvestlands* in the Upper World, it was about a village of tiny people deep in the undergrowth, and the star was a talented rebel who refused to be bound by the community's rules and regulations!

The one thing that *was* certain was the show's title. It was called '*In a Nutshell*!'

After having dismounted their crystalids, the girls made their way through the feverish hubbub as well as they could.
As soon as they were recognised the crowds parted to let them through. After all, Jessica was the 'Guest-of-Honour' and would be sitting with the Queen! Of course, the 'Guest-of-Honour' was supposed to be anyone who had come up with the solution to the riddle carved into the two golden ammonites...but as nobody had, the honour had been awarded to Jessica.

The Manager of the '*M.H.C*', Gladwyn Thrift, greeted his special guests at the top of the rocky stairway. It was there, atop a splendid crystal pedestal, that the two treasured ammonites had been put on display for everyone to inspect.

Mr Thrift, a portly gentleman with a shining bald head and a distinguished, silver moustache, bowed with a flourish before the two young ladies. Jessica and Jane courtseyed.
"I welcome you both!" he smiled, as he came out of his gracious bow. "The Queen is already in her seat. The show will commence as soon as the audience is seated!"
"We are both looking forward to the entertainment!" beamed Jessica, determined to hide her worries. "I believe it is Dillip Penlop's best work so far! We have much to look forward to!"
"We have indeed!" said the Manager. "But I have a small favour to ask before you enter the theatre! We have a little time!"
Jessica nodded politely, wondering what was coming.
"Yes, of course, Mr Thrift!"
"I wonder if you could be so gracious as to judge the model-making competition that has been running since the last harvest? The entries are over here, just beyond your two ammonites!"

Instantly, Jessica's heart sank as she heard the word 'harvest' and images of Jamie and snakes sprung into her mind. Bravely

she fought against them and followed the rather round, waddling shape of Mr Thrift.
She glanced at the two ammonites on their pedestal and once again pictures flooded into her head...this time of '*Deer Leap*' cottage and her father. She could feel tears welling in her eyes. One trickled down her cheek and she quickly dabbed it away. She gritted her teeth and bit her lip. She just *had* to compose herself. This was an important occasion. She *mustn't* let her emotions get in the way!
By the time she had reached the model display she had just about recovered, and she and Jane keenly inspected and admired the work. The theme had been the '*Goldcrest*' and there were a couple of dozen splendid entries mostly fashioned from wood and beaten bark.

Their detail was superb, with wonderfully crafted ranks of oars and billowing, yellow sails. But the one that caught Jessica's eye was of the famous ship plunging through waves carved from crystal. It seemed to have captured movement more than the others.
"The craftsmanship of all the entries is of the highest order, and it is difficult to choose a winner!" Jessica enthused, eying all the models. "But...," she hesitated, to build up the tension, "I choose...*this one*!"
Cheering from the nearby crowd instantly filled the air, as the winning model-maker shyly made his way forward to receive his prize...a gold framed, water-colour painting of the '*Goldcrest*' by the renowned artist, Pixwith Stem.
"Thankyou!" said the winner, a young crystal-carver called Jude from Middle Floss.
"Your work is absolutely fantastic!" smiled Jessica, staring into the deep blue eyes of the fair-haired model-maker. "I only wish I could set eyes upon it every time I wake!"
"Then take it!" said Jude. "It is yours!"
"N..no! I c...couldn't!" Jessica stuttered, feeling her face blush.
Jude picked up his model and presented it to her.

"Treat it as a gift to you and your brother for all you have done for Queen Venetia and *Aqua Crysta*. You are both honoured and praised throughout our Land!"
Jessica, now feeling that she was going to burst out into floods of tears at any moment, took the crystal model in her arms and pecked Jude on the cheek.

"Thankyou! I will treasure it forever, and I'm sure Jamie will, too!
He loves models! He has shelves of them back at '*Deer...*!"
She stopped and stared at the model.
Again, images of Jamie, and adders, and her father flooded into her mind and she felt her heart sink, as she touched the delicately carved prow of the wooden ship.
Then, in a flash, within her imagination, the ship changed from one of wood to one fashioned from...woven, white feathers! Gone had the mast and the yellow sail. And instead was an overflowing cargo of juicy, purple wimberries! And at the prow were two tiny figures!
"Jamie and Lepho!!" she suddenly called out to the complete surprise of Jude, Jane, Mr Thrift and the crowd! "It's Jamie and Lepho! They're on their way back home!!"
Everyone was utterly taken aback and utterly confused. To them the ship had remained exactly the same.
Jane put her arm around her friend and led her away from the puzzled eyes.
"I saw them!" Jessica whispered, tear traces glistening on her cheeks.
"It was *them*! I saw them! They're safe! They'll be back soon! You just watch!"
She looked down at the model in her arms. The feathers, the wimberries, Jamie and Lepho had all vanished. It was back to being the miniature '*Goldcrest*' again. Jane gave her a hug and together they walked into the vast auditorium. Strangely and magically a spring had returned into Jessica's step and she felt happier. But not until she saw Jamie in the flesh would she be satisfied that he was safe and well...but at least now she could try and enjoy the show!

The *Meeting Hall Cavern* looked magnificent!
The whole great, pink and white hollow packed from floor to ceiling with items brought down from the *Harvestlands* during the Upper World Spring and Summer. Giant ferns swept up the sides, their bright green tips lapping the stalactites that clung to the roof. Foxgloves towered between them, each purply-pink flower easily capable of holding at least a couple of Aqua Crystans. They seemed huge and really convinced the audience they were actually deep in tangled forest undergrowth. Creamy orange honeysuckle wove amid the stems with its heady scent filling the cavern. Flushes of blue speedwell, forget-me-not and bluebells edged behind the great crescent of seats between the pink stalagmites. Yellow primroses, dandelions and celandines filled one corner hiding the stems of the ferns and another corner overflowed with red poppies, campion and dog-roses. Harebells and buttercups peeped out everywhere and the floor was carpeted with daisies, creeping purple self-heal, violets and red and white clover.

It was all so lush and fresh looking and a great credit to the Aqua Crystans who had built the scenery. They had also constructed a village in the middle of the vast arena, with the fronts of half-a-dozen, conical, thatched cottages with round, curtained windows and red and blue doors. A grey, stone bridge arched over a shimmering make-believe stream and a bonfire pile of nutshells looked ready to light. Behind them was a tall, craggy rock, draped in mosses with a winding staircase leading up to a flat platform scattered with music stands and little crystal lights dangling on threads from splinters of wood...obviously the place for the orchestra!
And directly above, believe it or not, was a host of winged insects twirling on invisible threads, their outspread, still wings glinting in the crystal light...iridescent blue and emerald green dragon and damsel flies...even amber bees and hornets...all found dead on the forest floor by the scenery foragers! There were even ladybirds dotted around the greenery...Jessica counted at least twenty!
The whole effect was to dwarf the audience and take them into the Upper World. The splendid scene was certainly set for the show's 'First Act', and the buzz of the audience gradually faded as the members

of the orchestra began to file in from both sides. The excited anticipation of the audience...almost the whole population of *Aqua Crysta*...was almost tangible, as eager eyes, ears and noses sensed what was about to happen. They could hardly wait, as thudding hearts raced and darting glances probed this way and that into the rich scenery. They had waited many, many harvests for this moment...and now it was upon them!
Let the show begin!!

The brightest of the stage-light crystals were dimmed by oak leaves being slowly moved in front of them. The centre of the arena grew dark, except for the windows of the cottages and the little lights of the orchestra above, twinkling like stars. The silhouetted conductor raised his baton and a simple tune on a single woodwind instrument drifted around the cavern. The sound was both rich and melodic. The notes captured everyone. They were beautiful.
More wind instruments joined in and then a gentle pulse of percussion on hollow twigs and snail shells led to a choir of villagers entering the arena from between the flower and fern stems. They were humming to the simple woodwind tune and walking slowly into their village, hidden beneath the lush, overhanging undergrowth. As they continued humming, they set about their daily tasks...building the fire, cleaning clothes in the stream, repairing thatched roofs. Some were gently combing and plaiting children's hair, some just resting on patches of moss. The whole scene was one of peace and tranquility.
Then to everyone's surprise...one of the cottage doors opened...a red one... and out stepped the composer of '*In a Nutshell*' himself...Dillip Penlop! White bearded and dressed in a scarlet gown which reached the floor, he glided forward as the music faded. The vast *M.H.C.* fell silent, every pair of eyes fixed on the genius. What was he going to do or say?
The audience held its breath.
Dillip looked into the sea of expectant faces before him, smiled...and began...

Slowly spoken words pierced the silence, each one as clear as crystal, despite the sheer magnitude of the cavern dwarfing the

tiny speaker. Each word was savoured and relished by the captivated listeners as pictures were painted on the blank canvasses of their imaginations. They were entranced, in another world!
This is what they'd waited for!
Jessica glanced at Queen Venetia to one side of her and at Jane on the other. They were both intently gazing at the man in the scarlet gown and listening to his every utterance...

"Deep, deep, deep, in shady depths of green,
Where crushing footfalls have never been.
Beyond crowds of bustling, thorny tangles,
Stinging nettle and matted brambles.
In depths so deep that no man disturbs,
Where bluebell tinkles can just be heard,
And probing paths cannot lead eyes to see,
Forget-me-nots never to memories plea...

All at once, beneath towering beeches,
Amid the deepest, darkest reaches,
By curly fronds of fern which gently sway,
And lap the toes of walnut trees all day...
There a dappled sunlit patch secretly nestles,
Where stems and roots have never wrestled.
A rounded plot of mellow, mottled hues,
Where velvet moss, silky grasses fuse.

So bare a heart of calm confusion,
Yet well castled from all intrusion.
But, if you fought and won and braved the stings,
The scars and scratches, creepy crawly things,
And softly kneel with no rustling bracken,
Not one twig snappin' and crackin'.
Then through the last defences breathless peer,
Within your gaze, strange sights app...!"

The entrancing flow of Dillip's magical words was suddenly broken, to the complete surprise of everyone! The pictures he was painting in their minds were shattered...wiped out at a stroke!
What had happened?
A concerned buzz of whispering swept around the arena.
Did he want a drink of water?
Had he suddenly been overtaken by an outbreak of nerves?
Worse still, had he forgotten the next line?
The audience sat and wondered.
So too, did Queen Venetia, Jessica and Jane.
All three of them stared at the little genius.
What was going to happen next?
Mr Thrift, the Manager, looked a little worried, too!
Was the whole thing going to be a disaster?
Sweat poured from his forehead, and he twiddled his fingers.

Then...what was going to happen next...*happened*!!

Dillip suddenly raised his arms!
All at once, his stretched scarlet gown made him look enormous!
The whispering stopped instantly as though it had been turned off by a switch! Mr Thrift's fingers froze in mid-twiddle!
Then...the genius slowly lowered his left arm...and pointed towards the cavern's vast entrance.
A look of horror mixed with wonder crossed his face...and everyone in the audience turned nervously and followed his anguished gaze...
and then...
...they *all* saw it!!!

Chapter 7

Beyond the milky, pink light of the *Meeting Hall Cavern* entrance...in the Floss Cavern itself...was a shape!
A strange, sleek shape, the like of which nobody had ever set eyes on before! It had secretly arrived while all senses and minds had been engaged by Dillip Penlop's performance. No one had noticed it. There had been no warning...not even from *Lumina*, the eternal candle-flame!

Slowly and anxiously, every single Aqua Crystan stood and stared at the unwelcome visitor...although, thankfully, it didn't appear at all threatening nor hostile. It was white, smooth and soft...and almost graceful!
Suddenly, the shape glided further forward, revealing more of its trim outline.
The collective gasp of the audience was as though the *M.H.C.* itself had taken a gigantic intake of breath!
"What is it?" whispered Jessica to Queen Venetia.
The puzzled Queen shook her head, wishing her trusted advisor, Lepho, was by her side.

Then, before she could utter a sound, a joyous call exploded from the centre of the arena. It was Dillip.
"It's a feather! A white feather!" he shouted, his words echoing around the cavern. Another shocked gasp from the audience filled the air. Eyebrows raised and looks of surprise and curiosity crossed the faces of the Aqua Crystans, accompanied by knowing glances and smiles!
It had suddenly occured to them!

Of course! It was all part of the show!
A brilliant piece of drama conjured up by Dillip Penlop!
A wonderful spell of trickery that had fooled them all!
Although, it has to be said, *nobody* knew for sure!
But if it *was*...then it was a *master* stroke by the little genius!
And whoever had come up with the amazing special effect hovering outside the *M.H.C.* had also done a superb job!
Just then, something caught the eye of the entire audience! Movement at the front of the strange shape...the feather!...if it was a feather!
Two tiny figures could be seen!
Two tiny figures, one shorter than the other, both fiery haired!!
Two figures dressed in heathery purple!
Two figures waving energetically!
The Queen looked at Jessica and Jessica looked at the Queen!
It couldn't be...*could it*??
It *was*!! And moments later, at the entrance to the *M.H.C.*,
Queen Venetia was re-united with her trusty Mayor of Pillo and Jessica was in floods of tears as she threw her arms around her brother!
Lepho quietly informed the Queen of the tragic loss of life in the Upper World, and for the moment it was decided to say nothing to the assembled Aqua Crystans.
"I thought I'd never see you again!" sobbed Jessica as she squeezed the breath out of Jamie. "I could hardly believe it when I saw the adders...!"
"But *how* did *you* see the adders?" gasped Jamie.
"I'll tell you all about that lat...!" laughed Jessica.
"OK, OK...but first I've got to tell you our news!" burst her brother, at

last breaking free. “The ammonites...we’ve cracked the mystery!”
“You mean...we’ve *almost* ‘cracked it’, as you put it!” interrupted Lepho, glancing at the golden fossils on their crystal pedestal. “We still have some way to go! We still haven’t worked out the mysterious message...!”
“But we reckon that it’s all something to do with *Whitby*!” beamed Jamie.
“How did you work that out?” puzzled Jessica.
“Well, first we’ve seen scores of gulls from the coast while we were up in the *Harvestlands*, not to mention their feathers!” grinned Jamie, looking over his shoulder at his peculiar transport, “...and second, we’ve seen that whole vicious gang of adders!”
For a moment Lepho and Jamie looked a touch uncomfortable and became a little quiet. Memories of the fatal snake attack were still strong.
“I can see what you mean about Whitby and the gulls!” wondered Jessica.
“But what have adders got to do with it?”

By now, a crowd had gathered around the travellers as Lepho began to tell the story of the plague of naders (as he called them) that had terrified the ancient village of Whitby centuries ago when the Abbey had just been built.
“...It was the head of the Abbey, a lady called Hilda, who drove the serpents over the Whitby cliffs to their deaths. And legend has it, that as they perished, they curled and coiled into the form of ammonite fossils!”
“So that’s the second connection with Whitby!” insisted Jamie. “And Lepho reckons that both are clues to where dad is! Whitby is full of gulls and ammonite fossils!! It couldn’t be clearer! We’ve got to go there!”
“I agree!” said the Queen, with a note of concern in her voice. “The two of you shall venture there as soon as possible, in the Quest to find your father...!”
The crowd instantly cheered.
She raised her arms and the cheering ceased.
“But as for the show...!” she said solemnly...
The crowd looked dismayed.

Surely it wasn't going to be cancelled!
"If Mr Dillip Penlop and Mr Gladwyn Thrift give their consent...!" she went on gravely...and then...as a twinkling smile crept across her face...she joyfully exclaimed, "The show *will go on*!!"

As Jessica and Jamie climbed aboard Rudolph, Jane asked for the umpteenth time if she and her brother Jonathan could travel with them to Whitby.
"You know that Jonny's in the show!" said Jessica quietly. "He'd be ever so disappointed if he had to drop out! You go back in there and watch him and look after my gift from Jude! We'll soon be back!"

So, as distant musical notes could just be heard drifting from the cavern, Rudolph hovered in the warm, scented air and then gracefully turned towards Pillo. Queen Venetia, Lepho and Jane waved from the quayside and wished the venturers good fortune in their Quest. And there was no doubt about it, they would *certainly* need it!

If only they had known what was yet to come!

Chapter 8

By the time the Second Act was beginning back in the *Meeting Hall Cavern*, Jessica and Jamie were already about to set out on their long journey from the deserted and rather eerie Pillo. As warm applause rewarded the dancers and acrobats who were performing in the *M.H.C.*, Jessica glanced around the crystal room that had been home since she and her brother had arrived in *Aqua Crysta.*

"I'll miss my cosy little bed!" she sighed, as she gently stroked the beautiful jay feather that swept from the floor, through the knot-hole in the table and up to the ceiling.

"Chance of a spot of kip in *my* bed would be a fine thing!" mumbled Jamie, as he carefully folded the drawing he'd made of the golden ammonites and their mysterious messages.

"Are you sure you don't want a nap before we leave? You must be exhausted!"

"No, I'm ready for action! The sooner we get going the better! We've a heck of a way to go!"

They'd changed from their simple Aqua Crystan smocks and beaten bark sandals into the clothes they'd arrived in during the Upper World Summer. Jessica had kept them carefully folded in a chest in a rocky cranny at the back of their cave. It certainly seemed strange to be suddenly wearing their familiar old clothes from *Deer Leap*...yellow T-shirts, red anoraks, blue denim shorts, socks and fluorescent trainers

with the tiny lucky jay feathers still woven into their laces. They'd even found some coins in their anorak pockets...about seven pounds' worth in all. Could be handy for a drink and a snack in Whitby, they'd reckoned!
"You know it's going to be a bit nippy, don't you?" said Jessica looking at her bare legs. Winter's just round the corner...it must be October or even November up there!"
"Just keep your fingers crossed the Sun's shining when we get to the top of the well!" suggested Jamie. "The days were pretty mild during the foraging expedition, but the nights were chilly. We had camp-fires every single night!"

The plan was to travel by crystalid from Pillo to the place near the Larder Caves where the rope was still dangling from the bottom rung of the well's rusty, old, iron ladder. Then, if good fortune was with them, they would climb up through the mists, return to Upper World size, reach the well top and emerge into the Forest. Jamie would then use Tregarth's silent flute to summon the roe deer, Chandar and Strike, who would carry them to within easy walking distance of Whitby!
That was *it*!
That was the plan!
But *you all* know what happens to *plans*!
And so did Jessica and Jamie!
They just had to put trust in luck...fate...magic...or whatever they could cling on to! They had set their hearts on seeing their father and *Deer Leap* again! And something told them that sheer determination would win through in the end! It just *had to*!

"Now, are you sure you've got your sketch of the ammonites and the silent flute?"
Jamie slapped his back pocket.
"Sure have!"
"Then let's get the show on the road!"
They stepped out onto the terrace and gazed over the empty town.
Not a single soul could be seen. It seemed so quiet.
All four *Quats* of Pillo were deserted, even *Olde Quat* with its normally buzzing Market Square and little harbour-side cafes.

Even the huge, sweeping arc of the Pillo Falls precipice just hosted three or four trickles of water. The sound of them plunging into the shallow Floss below was all the children could hear.
"Isn't it quiet?" whispered Jessica in keeping with the tranquility.
Jamie nodded as he untethered Sabre and stroked its rainbow neck.
The crystalid seemed glad to see Jamie and began quivering its sets of transparent wings.
"I suppose it hasn't had much exercise while I've been away!"
"You're joking!" laughed Jessica. "I've ridden Sabre almost as much as Rudi! Jane and I have been all the way to Galdo Island on the crystalids about a dozen times! It's been brill!"

In next to no time the two children were gliding along the Floss Cavern and passing the entrance to the *Cave of Torrents.*
"Wish we could take a trip along there to *Torrent Lodge*!" smiled Jamie, as they flew over Knapweed's Crystal Mill.
"Oh, and why is that, then? As if I didn't know!" laughed Jessica.
"I'm just feeling a bit peckish, that's all! And that Megan Magwitch grub is absolutely *deee...licious*!" drooled Jamie, thinking about heather tips dipped in hazelnut cream and toasted sweet chestnut smothered in wimberry sauce, a couple of choice items off the *Lodge* menu!
"I think we ought to press on!" said Jessica. "We can both have a snack when we get up there to the Forest. There's plenty of tinned supplies hidden at *Old Soulsyke*, and we've got to call there anyway to get our jeans and pullies! Let's hope they're safely in the chest where we kept them in Summer!"

Soon, the pair of crystalids were flying through the Narrows and then past Middle Floss hamlet. Shortly afterwards, near the foot of the winding steps that led up to the Larder Caves, they spotted the dangling rope that would take them into the Upper World via the magical mists and the well.
And it was at that very same moment that Jessica suddenly realised that they had totally forgotten about *how* they were going to get up to the bottom of the well!
"No! No! No!" she exclaimed angrily. "How could we have been so *stupid*? It's going to delay us for ages!!"

Aqua Crystans were needed...about twelve of them...to tug on one half of the dangling rope! And where were all the Aqua Crystans? Watching the show at the *M.H.C.*!

"We'll just have to wait!" said Jamie, as they tethered Rudolph and Sabre to a handy wooden rail. "As soon as the show's over, there'll be boat loads of folk coming this way!"

"But the show could go on...and on! We could be stuck here for...!"

Suddenly Jessica heard a noise coming from the Larder Steps.

"What's that? Can you hear something?"

They both listened.

"Footsteps! It's footsteps! We're in luck!" burst Jamie.

"But everybody's at the...!"

"Oh no they're not! It's the foraging party I was with in the Forest! They must have finished storing away all the harvest we collected!"

It certainly was a stroke of good fortune! The arrival of Clem and the rest of the foragers couldn't have been better timed! And there were just enough of them to pull on half of the rope while, first Jamie, and then Jessica, rode on the driftwood seat up into the mists.

As Jamie clung onto the well ladder's seventh rusty rung, he gazed down and still could hardly believe what he was witnessing! It seemed so incredible! But there it was, once again, before his very eyes! As the thick rope jerkily slithered over the bottom rung, his sister's hand and red anorak sleeve suddenly plunged through the mist. Her hand grabbed the rung and she pulled herself up.

The magic had worked again!

They were both back to being full-size and hadn't noticed a thing!

Quickly, Jessica threaded the rope down into the magical world they had left behind. It was amazing to think that they were just a jump away from the tiny group of Aqua Crystans and Rudolph and Sabre on the shores of the River Floss! Yet everything suddenly seemed a whole world away, as if it didn't exist at all! No show at the *M.H.C.*! No little house in Pillo! No Lepho, nor Queen Venetia!

It was an incredible feeling!

Saddened by leaving *Aqua Crysta*, but at the same time cheered by thoughts of being on their way to finding their father and

Deer Leap, the children began the climb to the top of the well.
The going was tough as they pulled themselves up from one rung to the next into the darkness. They were soon sweating even though the air was cooling, the higher they climbed. But just moments later they were level with the door that led to the *Forest Cellar.* As they rested, happy images of the toy fairground and the giant dolls' house fluttered through their minds. It seemed such a long time since they'd first pushed the door open and discovered the hidden treasures!
As Jessica perched on the ledge in almost complete blackness, Jamie heaved himself up towards the slab of stone that separated one world from the other. He steadied himself, reached up and grasped the rough, gritty edge of the stone.
Slowly, it grated open.
There was no sudden flood of bright daylight.
It was dark and unwelcoming.
Icy air licked Jamie's fingers.
He shivered and pulled himself up until his eyes were level with the forest floor.
Yes, it *was* cold.
It was bitter!
But then...he noticed something that sent another sort of shiver down his spine. This time not one caused by the chilly air.
He blinked and looked again.
It was still there!
He could hardly believe his eyes!
It was the very *last* thing he wanted to see as he crawled out into the Upper World!
And his heart sank!

Chapter 9

The pile of glowing white crystals was about the size and shape of a glassy molehill that had erupted from a drift of pine needles beneath a towering spruce tree. It was a sight the children knew only too well!

One that took them straight back to the Summer day when *Deer Leap* and their father had vanished. They'd seen a similar heap of crystals amid the desolate foundations of their cottage. It had slowly dissolved to reveal the two golden ammonites. The work of the *Shym-ryn*.

"I sensed the *Shym-ryn* were about during the adder attack!" whispered Jamie, his teeth beginning to chatter. "When the snakes were suddenly snatched away and tossed into the trees. It was as if invisible hands had grabbed them by their tails!"

"But why would they try to save you?" asked Jessica. "They're not supposed to be on our side!"

"Well, I'm sure it was them!" insisted Jamie. "Lepho and I both saw wisps of purple mist...and the air went chilly!"

The children looked anxiously into the blackness between the trees!

Were they being watched?

Would they be followed through the Forest, like in the Summer?

"I wonder if that's why it's cold now!" thought Jessica. "Is it because it's getting on for winter...or is it the *Shym*...?"

All at once, the children gasped as the crystal heap began to dissolve, like a pile of ice-cubes by a roaring fire.
Just the same as in Summer.
Would another message carved into ammonites be revealed?
They waited and watched, becoming colder and colder by the second.
Soon, through the melting crystals, they could just make out the familiar outlines of curves and spirals!

And they were golden!
The children looked at one another and then back at the fossils.
This time there were *three* ammonites...and each had a single word carved across its coil.
But there were no cryptic codes to crack!
The words were in plain English!
As the glow from the remaining crystals faded, they could just make them out.
"*The...Golphin...Awaits.*" whispered Jamie.
"What the heck does *that* mean?"
"I haven't a clue but it's getting a touch spooky around here!" replied Jessica, recalling her last face-to-face encounter with a *Shym-ryn* in the attic of *Old Soulsyke.* "Let's get going!"

Together they dragged the stone over the top of the well and then Jamie blew on Tregarth's silent flute. Of course, not a sound could be heard and they just hoped Chandar and Strike would magically appear. As the last light from the crystals was extinguished, the children sat in the dark and waited.
"Do you think we ought to take the ammonites with us?" asked Jamie, as he traced one of the carved words with his forefinger.
Jessica shook her head.
"I think they'll just be extra weight to carry...and I reckon we can remember what the message is, whatever it means!"
" '*The Golphin*' sounds like a boat to me!" whispered Jamie. "Perhaps there's a boat waiting for us in Whit...!"
"Ssh! Ssh! What's that?" burst Jessica as quietly as she could, pointing into the almost pitch blackness between the trees.

A couple of twigs cracked.
"Someone's coming!" she burst again, stifling a scream.
She grabbed hold of Jamie, making him almost jump out of his skin!
"Calm down, sis! Calm down!" he whispered. "It could be Chandar and Strike! We don't want to scare 'em off!"

He was right. It was the two young roe deer, one albino and one darkish brown. The mysterious magic had summoned them once again and gently they nuzzled the children, as if renewing their friendship. In return, Jessica and Jamie stroked their sleek necks, grateful that the magic had brought them together again.

Moments later, as the deer nimbly sped across the Forest, with their passengers aboard, the sky began to clear. The heavy darkness was banished as clouds were swept away, and, slowly but surely, oceans of stars came into view beyond the tree-tops, casting milky starlight through the branches. And then, as one, particularly ponderous, but silver-lined cloud was pushed away, a perfectly round full moon sailed majestically into one of the oceans. The Forest was suddenly flooded with silvery light and the way ahead could be seen clearly through the narrow avenues of spruce and larch. The deer even seemed to canter and dance more quickly over the pine-needle drifts, as though the moonlight had made them more sure-footed. In no time, the children had crossed the *Harvestlands* and could just make out the crumbling walls of the abandoned farmstead that had been their secret den for over a year.

At *Old Soulsyke* they stopped for a bite to eat and to put on their jeans and warm pullovers. Jamie quickly opened a can of baked beans from their hidden 'survival kit' food supply, and poured them into a small saucepan. A minute later, a welcome ring of blue flames spluttered from the little gas-stove and the children gratefully warmed their hands. Jessica opened a tin of peaches and a couple of fizzy orange drinks and they quietly enjoyed a feast in the old kitchen.

"Not quite the same as crunchy flakes of sycamore keys in rowan berry jelly or toasted beech nut fingers in dandelion dip!" smiled Jamie, as he tucked into his hot beans. "But I'm glad we hid all this grub and it hasn't been raided by the local inhabitants!"
"You mean badgers and foxes armed with tin openers!" giggled Jessica, imagining a midnight feast attended by all the animals of the Forest, all helping themselves to everything in their secret larder. "I can just see the weasels serving up the meatballs in tomato sauce...!"
"And the squiggles passing round the ginger nuts!" laughed Jamie.
"And here come the first guests!" Jessica beamed, pointing to the front doorway. "They must have smelled the beans!"
Chandar and Strike, side by side, had stepped in from the farmyard! Then, as bold as brass, they strutted into the old kitchen, just like a pair of show ponies, heads held high and without the tiniest hint of nerves! The gentle tap-tap of their dainty hoofs on the stone-slab floor echoed between the walls of the old farm, and when they paused in a patch of silver moonlight they looked truly magical...especially Chandar!
She was so white!
Almost dazzlingly so!
"Isn't she beautiful?" Jessica whispered, getting to her feet and putting her arms around the young deer's neck. "She's so soft!"
Jessica stroked Chandar's silvery white forehead and looked into her huge eyes. Their strange, pinky-red glow made the deer seem to be even more magical.
"They're like rubies in fallen snow!" she smiled, in a world of her own.
Jamie by now was stroking Strike and thinking about their visit to *Old Soulsyke* during the Summer.
"Do you remember the *Shym-ryn* trapping us upstairs with that thick, glassy, crystal stuff over the trapdoor?" he mumbled, staring at the black hole in the ceiling. "We couldn't break it, however hard we stamped on it!"
"Albino rabbits and mice have pure red or pink eyes, too!" Jessica went on dreamily.
"And do you remember *Spook* the cat coming into the kitchen, twitching her tail and changing everything back into the 1950s?" Jamie recalled.

"Something, I think, to do with a lack of colouring pigment in their fur and eyes!"
"And then that spacecraft landed in the farmyard and that alien with the green head stepped out and kidnapped me...!"
"Jamie, what *are* you talking about? What alien?"
"You haven't heard a word I've said, have you?" burst Jamie.
"Yes I have!" replied Jessica calmly, at last snapping out of her dream world. " Something about an alien...in the 1950s...with pink eyes!"
They both laughed and offered the deer a juicy peach slice each.
The deer sniffed politely, but didn't accept!
"Don't suppose they're used to peach slices!" beamed Jessica. "Come on, it's time to get the show on the road again! Let's get going!"

Five minutes later, the deer and their riders were speeding over the pine-needles beneath the silvery moon, past the fallen barn and by the old quarry. Soon they were at the spot where *Deer Leap* should have been.
For a moment both children wished that the magic had been reversed and that the cottage and their father were both back safe and sound. They imagined the front door opening and Mr Dawson marching out and greeting them, with the tuneful, musical sounds of '*Penny Lane*' or '*Hey Jude*' by the Beatles, following him into the moonlight.
But no such luck!
There was still nothing there...just a scattering of sad, old foundation stones. The *Shym-ryn's* vengeful magic still held the cottage and their father in its clutches.

The children bit their lips, gritted their teeth...and rode off into the chilly night. Whitby was just a couple of hours away...maybe just one, if everything went as planned!
Soon, they would put everything right!
Soon, they'd be back in *Deer Leap*...with their dad...even with his loud 1960s music!
But life is full of the unexpected ruining the best laid plans...

...if only they'd known what lay round the next corner!
Tragedy and more heartbreak were about to strike yet again!

Chapter 10

William Hoggett's alarm had gone off at precisely 2am...as it always did. It had buzzed just twice but had done its job. William opened one bleary eye after the other, swept back his side of the duvet and tiptoed out of the bedroom without disturbing his gently snoring wife, her head a perilous, threatening mass of huge, lime green hair-curlers and her face totally disguised by a hefty helping of plastered cucumber face-cream!

The middle-aged couple had lived in their small terraced house on the edge of the city of Bradford, Yorkshire, for many, many years...for almost as long as William had worked for '*Tosko*', the biggest supermarket company in the country...if not the World!

Holding his breath, in case his wife should awake, he'd crept downstairs and into the kitchen. It was more than his life was worth to disturb her at that time in the morning! Imagine the cursing wrath of a woken woman made even more horrific by that vicious, spiky, warrior head-dress and that matching warrior war-paint! Definitely not a risk worth taking!

Once in the safety of the kitchen, he'd breathed again, poured himself a bowl of *Tosko's 'Weetie Crispies'*, brewed a mug of *Tosko's 'Super Sup Super Tea'* and popped a slice of *Tosko's 'Wholemeal Wonder White'* into the toaster. As he sat at the kitchen table sipping his tea, he gazed through the window and up at the bright full moon that sailed high

above the city skyline. It looked beautiful and tinged all the rooftops with silver.
'It'll be bright o'er them moors tonight!' he'd thought to himself, as his mind wandered off to the working day ahead. He knew that at three o'clock on the dot, in the dead of the night, he would be on his way from the giant depot. Creeping away, along deserted highways. Stealing away, across the peaceful, sleeping, moonlit Yorkshire countryside. And, best of all, he'd be with the love of his life... his other woman...*Beryl*!!...his beloved set of wheels!!
William, you see, was a lorry-driver and he just loved his job on the open road, delivering goods to *Tosko* stores all over Yorkshire.
And today, Friday, was the best day of the week! It was the run to Whitby and Scarborough on the Yorkshire Coast...and that took him on his most favourite road of all...the twenty-odd miles over the wonderful, North Yorkshire Moors!
As he'd buttered his toast with *Tosko's 'Do You Think It's Margarine?'* and then spread it with *Tosko's 'Extra Thick Cut, Extra Tangy, Extra Orange Marmalade Extra'* he considered the venture ahead with relish. He could hardly wait to set out into the chilly night.
So, at just after twenty-past two in the morning, the rather bulky figure of Mr Hoggett had pulled on his winter jacket and woolly bob-cap, wrapped his scarf round his ample neck and had stepped out into the silent, silver street. He'd quietly closed the door behind him and had headed towards the depot, his footsteps echoing over the cobbles and paving stones.
He would be there in twelve minutes precisely.
He would turn *Beryl's* ignition key at exactly three o'clock.
And by five o'clock, if all went well, he'd be driving along that winding, weaving road that took him over the desolate moors to far-flung Whitby, the little town nestled snugly on the rugged coast, like a giant swallows' nest clinging to the cliffs on the very edge of Yorkshire.

Meanwhile, under the same, beautiful Full Moon that William Hoggett had observed in Bradford, Jessica and Jamie made a fateful, and ultimately tragic decision. Instead of taking the track from

Deer Leap and then the narrow moorland lane, they decided to cut further across the Forest. If they'd taken the track and the lane then the tragedy that was about to happen would have been avoided.
It would never have happened.
But fate...the coming together of small instances in the lives of people and creatures who have never met one another, the unexpected crossing of solitary paths...is the mistress of both surprise and ill-fortune!
She was about to spring one of her devilish traps!

The time...although Jessica and Jamie didn't know it...was about a quarter-past-five. It was still dark. Chandar and Strike glided across the sprucelands as silently as ghosts. The children clung tightly around their soft, sleek necks, almost hugging them, and gripped their flanks with their knees. It was a bit like riding the crystalids in *Aqua Crysta*, but the deers' fur was much more comforting.

As the deer reached the boundary of the Forest they came to a wooden fence.
Just beyond was the road to Whitby.
Perhaps the deer could have jumped the fence with their passengers still on board, but they stopped and Jessica and Jamie dismounted.
The gentle animals grazed for a moment on the long grass by the thick fence posts. Strike even pushed his head through one of the gaps to reach some tender shoots on the other side.
Suddenly, without warning, they both sprang over the fence as though they'd been stung! Chandar first, and then Strike.
Quickly, Jessica and Jamie followed. They'd soon be back upon their trusty steeds and on their way over the moors to Whitby.
But...for some unknown reason...the pair of young deer kept on going!
It was as if they thought their riders were already on board!
"Come back! Come back!" called Jessica into the night.
Jamie even blew on the silent flute!
But all was to no avail!

The deer just kept on leaping higher and higher over the springy heather!
They almost seemed to be enjoying the extra bounce beyond the fence!
They were having fun!
The heatherlands certainly made a change from the less yielding pine-needle drifts of the Forest floor!
But it was then that the children realised that each frivolous, frisky, carefree bound was taking the magical deer...closer...and closer...
...to the road!

William Hoggett, equally carefree, was tapping his chubby fingers on his large steering-wheel to the rhythms of the music on his favourite all-night radio station. The journey from Bradford had been uneventful and the traffic very light.
He'd made it to the moors in good time. As he drove *Beryl* along, he gazed over the gently undulating landscape that was all beautifully dusted with silver moonshine. It was a splendid sight. The one he'd been thinking about ever since his alarm had woken him at 2am.
'Soon be at *Tosko's* in Whitby!' he thought, as he sucked on a mint and delighted in the glistening heatherlands that surrounded him.

Chandar and Strike gambolled closer and closer to the road. They were heading for a bulky, straggly gorse-bush that lay just by it. Behind them, by at least the length of a couple of cricket pitches, were Jessica and Jamie, struggling and panting through the deep heather.
The deer reached the gorse-bush and stopped for a moment, hidden from the road. An unfamiliar sound in the distance made their ears twitch.
The slender creatures stood alert, as still as statues.
The sound became louder and louder.
The deer were uncertain.
They looked at one another unsure of what to do!
Run back to the Forest, stay put...or panic onwards?

Then Jessica and Jamie caught sight of it, silhouetted against the silver moors, headlights beaming.
It was the lorry from Bradford...*Beryl*... cutting through the moonlit night on that same desolate stretch of black road that lay just before them!

William Hoggett, gripping his steering-wheel and travelling at about 50mph, leaned forward and twiddled with his radio dial. The reception had suddenly become a bit fuzzy. It always did at this particular spot over the moors. Perhaps it was the height above sea-level, or the fact that he was in the middle of nowhere.
He didn't even notice the straggly gorse-bush as he roared towards it.
Nor the albino deer!

Jessica and Jamie just stood up to their knees in heather and watched, horror-stricken!
There was nothing they could have done about it.
They were helpless.
"*No! No! No!*" screamed Jessica, squinting through the fingers over her eyes.

Whoosh!!
Fate's devilish trap was sprung!

At exactly the same instant as the lorry thundered past the gorse-bush, that innocent young creature, Chandar...made her last leap...straight into the hard, unforgiving steel that was the sturdy side of the vast lorry!
William Hoggett didn't even notice.
He'd neither seen, nor heard, nor felt anything!
The radio reception suddenly cleared and he headed on to Whitby, completely unaware of the collision.
Jessica and Jamie, unable to move, just stared at the still, white body

lying on the road. It was being gently nuzzled by Strike.
Tears welled in their eyes and poured down their cheeks.
They felt sick in the pits of their stomachs.
They trembled as they stood there, and their hearts sank yet again.
Could they go on after what had happened?
Or was this...the end of the Quest??

Chapter 11

As the lorry rumbled over the distant horizon and onwards to Whitby, its driver innocently unaware of the tragic death in its wake, the two children approached the roadside with heavy hearts. They couldn't believe what they had seen.

The wonderful animal that Jessica had spotted for the first time just after they'd arrived in Yorkshire, was dead. She thought of that day and how she, Jamie and her father had watched the perfectly still group of roe deer standing near their nameless cottage. She remembered them all suddenly springing away as the Land Rover moved slowly up the track. After that the cottage had a name...*Deer Leap*!

Chandar had been one of those deer, and around her neck had been a garland of blue jay feathers...a magical sign that there was something special about her. Not the first sign, of course! Even before that day, Jessica had seen images of the young albino in the vast Pegasus constellation in the night sky...jumping friskily over the stone walls of the Forest.

The lifeless, white body, glistening in the silver moonlight, lay half on the road and half on the short grass near the straggly gorse-bush. It seemed so strange to see her lying so still, her lively spirit gone forever. Her eyes were closed, the rubies lost. She almost looked as though she was sleeping, except there was no shallow,

tell-tale rising and falling of her soft, snowy sides.
There was no trace of blood.
The glancing blow from the lorry had killed her instantly. Her death had been quick, like that from a bolt of lightning. She hadn't suffered.

Jessica knelt down by her friend and gently stroked Chandar's slender neck, anger and guilt beginning to well up inside her.
"It's all our fault!" she whispered, tears still flooding from her eyes.
"We could have walked to Whitby! Then you would have been safe in the depths of the Forest!"
Jamie stroked Strike who looked all alone and sad, and not sure what to do.
"He's got to go back into the Forest!" sobbed Jessica. "We mustn't take him any further away from his home and *Aqua Crysta*. Besides, he must be missing Chandar terribly! They were inseparable!"

As if he understood every word, the young buck nuzzled his dead companion for one last time, turned and leaped away over the heather. He stopped once, glanced backwards, and then bounded over the fence and was gone, dissolving into the darkness. His life would never ever be the same again.
Jessica stroked Chandar's forehead and raised her eyes into the twinkling night sky where the great square constellation of Pegasus captured her tearful gaze. Once again, she saw pictures, framed by the corner stars.
The young albino deer again! This time, not leaping over walls in the Forest but dancing nimbly over the heathery moors towards the coast. The sea was shimmering in the background beneath a Full Moon and beyond the silhouetted remains of Whitby Abbey clinging to a cliff-top. She instantly thought of it as the spirit of Chandar, still alive, and guiding them onwards on their Quest.
It was the sign she wanted and *had* to follow!
They *must* carry on!

The task of moving the body from the roadside and hiding the deer beneath the gorse-bush was painful. It was also quite hard work. For such a light-footed creature, her dead-weight surprised

the children, and getting her away from the road and behind the bush took quite an effort.
"We will bury her properly later!" gasped Jessica, tugging up some bracken to conceal Chandar even more. "When we've completed our

Quest and everything's back to normal, we'll come here in the Land Rover and take her...and bury her in the Forest! OK?"
Jamie quietly nodded. He was beginning to have secret doubts about the whole venture, but he knew that they had to persevere despite the setbacks. His sister's determination and optimism spurred him on, together with the thought of seeing his father again.
Yes, they would succeed!
They *had* to...for Chandar's sake!!

Chapter 12

The journey beneath the stars to Whitby was uneventful. They kept to footpaths away from the main road and signposts guided them over the moors and then through a wooded valley with a narrow stream crossed by stepping-stones.

They made good progress and their fast walking kept them warm.

Beyond the hamlet of Littlebeck they had a rest and a drink at a lion's head fountain set in a stone wall.

"We must be well over half way there by now!" suggested Jamie, his hands cupped beneath the ribbon of water flowing from the lion's mouth.

"I reckon if we keep this speed up, we'll be in Whitby in a couple of hours! Then we can have some breakfast! I'm starving!"

Jessica laughed and ruffled her brother's untidy mop of ginger hair.

"We'll make sure your fuel tank's nice and full before the detective work begins. I must say I'm a bit peckish myself! I just hope we've got enough money to buy something!"

An hour later, via moonlit lanes, they rested on a great, arched steel bridge that spanned the width of the River Esk at Ruswarp village. Nearby were the first houses they'd come across in any number since leaving the Forest...silver cottages nestled around a church with a tall spire. Next to the bridge was a small railway station.
"Whitby's just round the corner!!" said Jamie, pointing down the river.

"How about following the railway line? It'll be the quickest and the easiest way, and there'll be no trains at this time of the morning!"
"I'm not sure about that!" replied Jessica, looking up into the streaky sky. "Dawn's about to break and there's bound to be an early train! No, I think we'd better stick to footpaths! Come on, let's go! The sooner we get to Whitby, the sooner we can get some grub!!"
The Sun had risen into a clear, blue sky by the time the children reached the seaside town. They walked down a gentle hill towards the harbour, both of them shattered and exhausted, not to mention...*starving*!!
And *food* was *definitely* on their minds as they collapsed onto a bench by a mountain of lobster-pots and near a splendid full-masted sailing ship called the '*Grand Turk*'.
They were in Whitby at last!! It had been one heck of a walk, and they were very pleased with themselves! They'd made it! Now the Quest could really begin, but *not* until they'd had a bite to eat!

Breakfast turned out to be a couple of scrumptious sausage-rolls and a couple of mouth-wateringly, magnificent cream-cakes, washed down with cold, fizzy ginger beer!

And, believe me, every single mouthful and every single swig was gratefully savoured! Never, in the whole history of breakfasts, had a breakfast been so welcome! Especially one perched on Whitby's

harbour-side, just next to its swing-bridge, looking over the gently lapping water and small, bobbing fishing boats towards the jumble of buildings that made Old Whitby on the east side of the River Esk. Above the red roofs, set against the sky, were the cliff-top St Mary's Church and the ancient ruins of Whitby Abbey.
The railway-station clock said it was just after nine and already the middle of Whitby was bustling with people.
"I wonder...what...day of the week it is?" said Jessica, licking the cream off her lips.
"Judging...by the number...of kids about," suggested Jamie, busily using a moistened forefinger as a magnet to make sure he devoured every flaky crumb of pastry in the sausage-roll bag, "I reckon...it's a week-end!"
"There's one way...to find out!" beamed Jessica, draining the very last drop from her ginger-beer can. "I'll just nip into that newsagent's over there!"
"What? And ask the guy what day it is?" laughed Jamie. "He'll think you're barmy!"
"No, you twit! I'll look on the front of a newspaper!"
A moment later she was back with a great smile across her face, almost from ear to ear!
"It's the half-term holiday! It's a Friday! And best of all...it's the last day of October! *Hallowe'en and all that*!!"

For the rest of the morning the children wandered around Whitby, looking for *anything* that might help them...*any* sort of clue! Many shop windows were decorated with fat, orange pumpkins with ghoulish faces carved out of them, while others displayed frightening skulls dripping with fake blood and draped with sticky spiders' webs!

There were couples and whole families walking about the narrow streets dressed in morbid, black, Victorian clothes, all with pasty white faces! Some even looked like *Count Dracula* himself, complete with fangs and blood-shot eyes! It was all pretty spooky! And *that* was during the day! Jessica and Jamie wondered what on earth the old town would be like after sunset!

All morning, herring gulls wheeled in the blue sky, their non-stop screeching reminding Jamie of the end of his *Harvest Expedition*! It seemed ages and ages ago since he was with Lepho in the Forest...and even more strange to think that he had been no taller than a pine cone!

Ammonites, of course, were everywhere! Not only did they feature in the Whitby town crest, but there were two gigantic, concrete seats shaped like ammonites near the swing-bridge! Fossil and gem shops had the real things piled in their windows...in all sizes! Some as tiny as 5p coins, some bigger than dinner-plates! Some were even sliced in half to reveal their beautiful, spiralling interiors with lots of compartments which became smaller and smaller as they spun to their centres. In between the ammonites were stacks of ear-rings and necklaces all set with shining, black droplets of polished 'jet'...another Whitby fossil...ancient pieces of wood from prehistoric monkey-puzzle trees!

By mid-day, of course, with all this '*wandering about*', the children were, once again, feeling a little peckish!
As they climbed a steep street called Flowergate, they spotted a little cafe called '*Sherlock's*'.
"How about a coffee and a cake?" suggested Jamie, as he leaned over an old fashioned bicycle, pressed his nose to the window and gazed at the

goodies to eat. "It looks fantastic inside! It's all Victorian! And the grub looks ace!"

"Must be something to do with *Sherlock Holmes*, the detective!" smiled Jessica. "And as, I suppose, *we're* a couple of detectives...then it's *definitely* the place for *us*!"

A moment later, they'd both stepped from the twenty-first century back to the late eighteen-hundreds. Nooks and crannies were full of old books, hat-stands, candlesticks and flowery ornaments...but, unfortunately, every single table was occupied.

"Plenty of space upstairs!" called a friendly lady from the counter, sounding like a conductress on an old double-decker bus. "We're very busy! What with half-term *and* Hallowe'en!"

The children shuffled between the tables, glancing at all the customers.

They all seemed to be dressed up in Victorian gear! Whiskered men in long coats and waistcoats with top-hats and walking-sticks, red cheeked women in billowing dresses with little feathery hats and parasols...and all the children seemed dressed to match! Then, of course, there were the spooky, pasty faced Gothic brigade, not to mention the *Count Dracula* and *Sherlock Holmes* look-alikes! It was like some kind of fancy-dress party! Jessica and Jamie felt a bit out of place in their anoraks, jeans and fluorescent trainers!

They squeezed to the back of the cafe past an ancient upright piano and several glass cases full of bracken and stuffed animals. Then up a narrow staircase, with walls crammed with dozens of fancy, gold-framed paintings, portraits and faded photographs, which led them to the first floor room.

There was just one vacant table left...in the corner next to a towering bookcase. Its shelves were absolutely packed to overflowing with not only ranks of thick, leather-bound books, but also brass oil-lamps, copper kettles, green glass bottles, black chunky typewriters and antique clocks with pearly faces. Jamie even spotted a model of a steam-engine and a real human skull!

As they sat, Jessica was captivated by the ornate fireplace opposite the bookshelf, its mantelshelf packed with even more books, candlesticks and oil-lamps. Above it, on the chimney breast, hung a huge, gilt-framed mirror reflecting the room's curtained windows. But it was one particular pile of three thick, leathery books that had caught her eye. They were lying on their sides, on top of one another, supporting a delicate china cup and saucer. She stared at the books intently, even as the young waitress appeared and asked for their order.

"And what would sir 'n madam like?"

"Two small coffees, please, with milk, and two slices of chocolate gateau!" gasped Jamie, poring over the menu, as though he was at *Torrent Lodge*! "Is that OK, sis?"

Jessica silently nodded, her eyes glued to the broad, tarnished brown spine of the lowest book of the aged trio.

For along it was another trio.
An enticing threesome!
One, two, three gleaming, golden ammonites in a neat row!
Jessica shivered as she felt the magic!
This is what they had been looking for!

This would lead them to Dad and *Deer Leap*!!
She was certain of it!
And, as she watched...the ammonites began to gently glow...
...as though they knew that she'd spotted them...
...and the special magic was working!!

Chapter 13

It was as though Jessica was being drawn to the pile of books by some kind of invisible thread! As though she'd been hooked by a magical spell cast by an unseen fisherman behind the fireplace! Round and round he wound his line in. His bait had worked! The glittering ammonites had glinted and caught Jessica's eye! Just like a shimmering fly on a hook could catch a hungry salmon in the River Esk! Silently, she crept across the room and gently fingered the three spiralling fossils. They weren't real but somehow stood out from the thick, brown spine of the lowest book. The book was called '*Nautilus*'.

Carefully, she lifted the cup and saucer and slid the book out from beneath the other two. It appeared heavy, but it almost seemed to glide from the mantelshelf with a peculiar lightness...as though it was delighted to have been chosen! The gilt ammonites continued to glow as she replaced the cup and saucer and made her way back to her seat, where Jamie had already introduced himself to four children sitting at the next table.

Lina, Molly, Caitlin and Cameron were all from Whitby and aged eleven

or twelve. Each was dressed splendidly for Hallowe'en, the girls in Gothic black silks and lace and Cameron as a young Sherlock Holmes with deer-stalker hat and matching cape!
Jamie had cleared a space on the table and spread out his drawing of the original pair of golden ammonites. The four children were curious to know the meaning of the letters.
"That's exactly what we're here to discover!" said Jamie, looking at Cameron. "Perhaps Sherlock Holmes can solve the mystery!"

"Well!" suggested Cameron, waving a huge antique magnifying-glass over the sketch. "It is obviously some sort of *code*...!"
There was a small round of applause from the girls, their sarcastic clapping slightly muffled by their black gloves.
"I could have told you *that*!" chirped Lina, her dark eye-brows almost raised to the rafters above her pale, powdered face.
"So...," continued Sherlock, totally ignoring the girls, "...the first thing to do...is to write down all the letters in a straight line, starting in the middle of the two ammonites!"
Meanwhile, Jessica sat down and inspected her ancient book, especially the tasselled, red leather bookmark that protruded slightly from its top. Carefully, she opened the book at the marked page. The Whitby children seemed interested in all this, too!

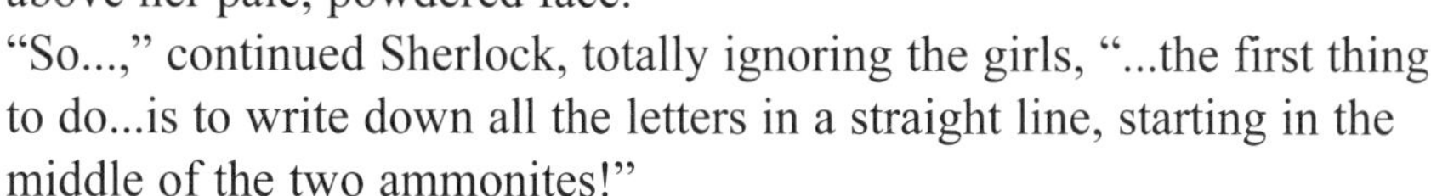

"Are you from round here? Never seen you before!" asked Caitlin politely, raising a black-netted veil, to reveal another chalky Gothic face.
"We're from Pillo!!" burst Jamie, without thinking.
"Pillo? Where's *Pillo*?" laughed Molly, sipping her hot chocolate. "Sounds like a place in a bedroom furniture store!"
"It's a small town in *Aqua Crysta*! Oww!" burst Jamie again, still

without thinking and this time receiving a sharp kick on the ankle from his sister!
The four Whitby children looked quizzically at one another.
"*Aqua Crysta*!" said Jessica, as cool as a cucumber, and gazing at the illustrations in the book. "It's a dump of a place near London! We're up here on our hols! Glad to be away from the smoke and the traffic! Whitby's brill! Do you live here?"
The children nodded and Jamie began to write the letters on a scrap of paper provided by Lina from her dainty, black-laced handbag, using a pencil borrowed from Sherlock Holmes' waistcoat pocket.
"That house is at the bottom of the famous *One-Hundred and Ninety-Nine Steps* that lead up to the Abbey...at the end of Church Street and the beginning of Henrietta Street!" said Caitlin, pointing to the large picture in the book.
Jessica smiled and nodded. She'd already noticed the three ammonites above the front door of the cottage in the illustration.
"Is that cottage still there?" she asked.
"It *was* the last time *I* looked!" quipped Molly with a grin. "I think it's called '*Spindle Top*'!"

At that moment, the waitress returned with the coffees and slices of gateau.
"'Ere, you two! You be careful with that book!" she said as calmly as she could. "In fact, I think you'd better put it back! We don't want coffee spillin' on it, do we?"
Jessica had seen and heard all she wanted.
She gently closed the book, returned it to the mantelshelf and replaced the cup and saucer.
Just as she sat down again a couple of Gothic adults appeared at the top of the stairs. A man and a woman, both resplendent in long, black coats, black buckled shoes and black headwear.
"Come on, kids! Have you finished? It's time to go!"
The four Whitby children stood up and said their goodbyes.

"See you at the fireworks tonight!" called Sherlock Holmes. "Keep the pencil! I'll come and claim it back when I'm next in *Aqua*...hmmm...*Crystal*?...or whatever it's called!"
"Have a spooky time!" laughed Caitlin, as the rest trooped down the stairs with a clatter. "And good luck cracking your secret code! Byeee!"

With that, the children vanished, and Jessica and Jamie nibbled their delicious slices of cake and sipped their coffees.
"That was a good idea from Sherlock Holmes!" mumbled Jamie as he completed copying all the letters from both ammonites.
When he'd finished he looked at them blankly.
"They still make no sense at all!" he grumbled.
Jessica glanced at the leather book on the mantelshelf.
The embossed, gilt ammonites twinkled back at her.
They seemed to be almost winking at her!
She looked at the lines of letters on the pieces of paper.
She gasped as certain letters seemed to stand out!
They were almost jumping out at her!
Excitedly, she pointed to them with a shaking forefinger!
One by one!!
Every *third* letter!!
"*W...H...I...T...*!!" she read, her eyes widening by the second.
"*Whitby*, *Yorks*!"
She looked at Jamie, grabbed the pencil and looked for another set of letters...every *third* one, starting from the '*H*'!
She put a dot over each letter.
"*H...I...L...D...A...*!!" Jamie gasped as he read out the letters.
"*Hilda Snakes*!"
"What the dickens does *that* mean?" burst Jessica.
Jamie thought for a moment.
"Just a minute! Hang on! It's coming!" he spluttered, closing his eyes tightly, then twisting and contorting his face as though he was wringing out some deeply buried item from his memory!

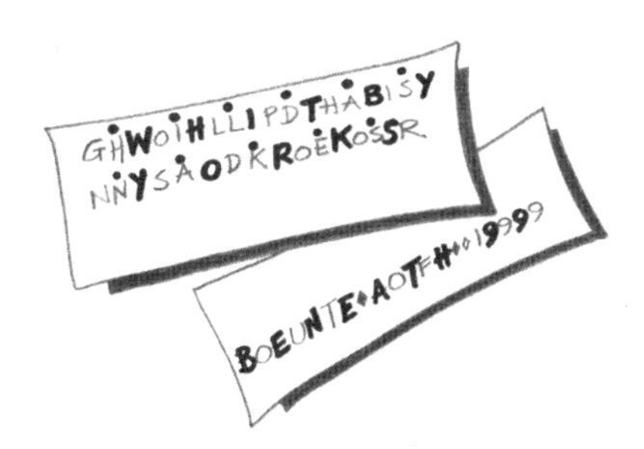

“That’s it! I’ve got it! I remember Lepho mentioning something about Hilda when we were attacked by those terrible adders on the *Harvest Expedition*!! That’s it! Hilda was in charge of Whitby Abbey...way, way back in time...and she got rid of a plague of adders by driving them over the cliffs...and, as they plunged into the sea...they curled up into spirals like ammonites!! That’s why they have ammonites on the Whitby town crest! *Hilda Snakes* must be *ammonites*!!”
“Three of them...like the three above the cottage door in the picture in the book!” whispered Jessica, beginning to make some sort of sense out of the mystery.
She glanced again at the golden spirals twinkling on the book spine above the fireplace.
Her eyes went back to the scrap of paper.
Again she followed every third letter, this time starting with the ‘*G*’!
“*G...O...L...P...H...*!!” she read, becoming more and more excited.
“*Golphin’s Door*!!”
“*Golphin*!!” exploded Jamie, nearly making all the other customers in the cafe jump out of their skins! “The same as on the ammonites at the top of the well in the Forest! *The Golphin Awaits*!!”
Jessica could hardly believe it!
They’d almost cracked the secret code. All the letters on one piece of paper had been used. But what was on the second piece?
The children stared at it as they mopped up the last crumbs of their slices of cake and drained the last drops from their coffee cups.
However much they stared, nothing appeared.
Jessica glanced at the book on the mantelshelf.
Even its golden ammonites had stopped shining.
Was the magic running out?
“We’ve just *got* to solve the *last line*!” she snapped, losing patience with herself. “*Where is ‘Golphin’s Door*’??”
Suddenly, Jamie pointed to the letters.
“It’s every *two* this time!!” he exclaimed, causing customers’ heads to twist round again and issue an angry, concerted ‘*Ssshhh*!’
“*Beneath...99*!!” he burst. “Then back to the beginning...*Out of 199*!!”
Jessica could hardly believe her ears!

"The *One-Hundred and Ninety-Nine Steps* that Caitlin was on about!" she called out, totally unaware that everyone in the packed upstairs room of the cafe was staring at her with looks of annoyance etched across their faces! "And we've got to find step number *Ninety-Nine*!!"

She looked up from the scraps of paper and saw the dozen-or-so irate faces glaring at her. The chattering and clinking of tea-cups and saucers had stopped. All was as quiet as a grave-yard. Jessica felt herself blushing and wishing that a great hole in the floor would swallow her up! How embarrassing!
Quietly, she nudged Jamie, and, amidst the stern, staring silence, the two of them quickly tidied the drawings and paper away and shuffled awkwardly to the top of the stairs.
Then, with a brief wave and a cheeky smile, they darted down the steps, paid their bill and...much to their relief, walked out into the weak October sunshine.

Now the *real* adventure could begin!!

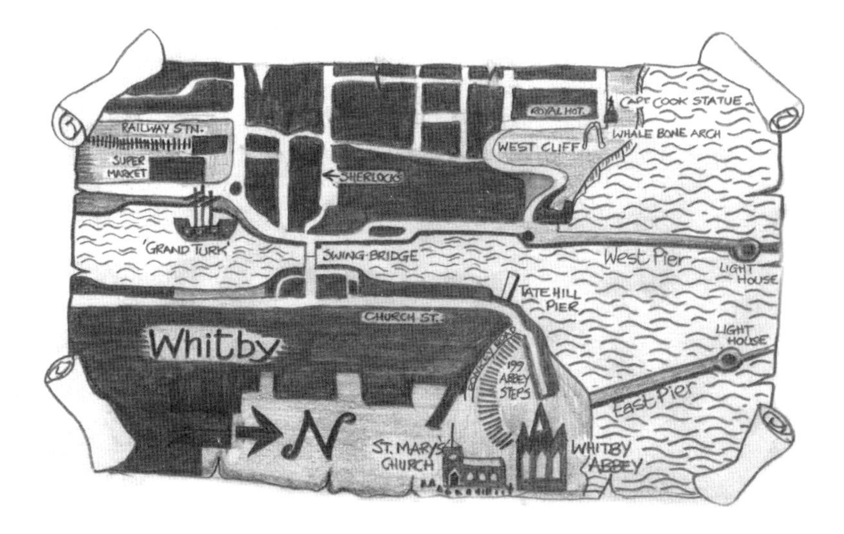

Chapter 14

By mid-afternoon, Church Street on the Old Side of Whitby was absolutely heaving with tourists and holiday-makers. It was quite warm for the end of October so many were dressed in colourful, summery clothing making those dressed in black Victorian gear stand out like sore thumbs!
Gift shops, jewellers and cafes were overflowing with folk from all over the world, all enjoying a spot of late Autumn sunshine before the onset of the cold months.
After crossing the swing-bridge (and touching the three ammonites on the town crest for luck) Jessica and Jamie ploughed through the hordes of people wandering along the narrow, cobbled street. They passed the small, bustling market-square, packed with cheerful stalls, then an old sandstone Victorian school opposite a red brick Wesleyan chapel that had become an arts and crafts centre. The narrow street became even narrower as it tapered towards a pub and a working jet factory and museum at the foot of the famous, rocky staircase.

"There's *Spindle Top* cottage!" pointed Jessica.

"And the three ammonites in the wall! Just like the picture in the book!"
They treated themselves to an ice-cream cornet each...'*99*'s, of course, with chocolate bars sticking out...and sat down on the fifth and sixth steps near a black lamp-post.
"Now we've got...a bit of counting to do!" slurped Jamie, as his tongue demolished his delicious, chilly whirl of glistening cream.
"Jamie, try and eat it with a touch of decorum, for goodness sake!" grumbled Jessica, delicately savouring her chocolate first. "You look as though you haven't had anything to eat for six months! There's people watching you!"

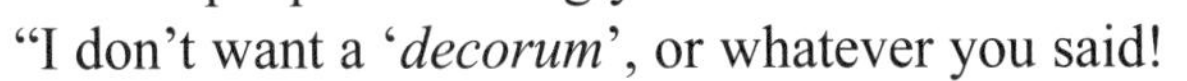

"I don't want a '*decorum*', or whatever you said! The chocolate will do!" insisted Jamie, now beginning to nibble his cornet. "*Ninety-Nines* have *chocolate bars* not '*decorums*'!!"
People were pouring up and down the famous worn steps which had been trodden for centuries by church congregations and visitors to the Abbey.
"It's a pity it's not one of those *excavator* things they have in super-stores and the London Underground!" considered Jamie as his chocolate bar disappeared. "It'd save folks' legs!!"
"You mean '*escalator*'!" laughed Jessica, looking at her brother vacuuming his ice-cream down his throat. "*Excavators* are those great big digging machines that can bite gigantic mouthfuls of earth...*a bit like you*!!"
"OK, OK, clever clogs!" said Jamie. "Whatever they're called, one would be very handy here...it looks one heck of a climb!"

The wide stone staircase wound up the side of the cliff to the church grave-yard at the top. Grass was on the left all the way, but on the right was a vertical drop down to a cobbled street called Donkey Road.

"C'mon, let's get going!" urged Jamie, after the last trace of his cornet had finally vanished. “And make sure you count in your head or we’ll get really mixed up! OK?”

So, the great climb began, and upwards they plodded, carefully counting the steps. After step number 47 there was a wide, flat, stone-flagged platform. They stopped and rested and looked over the red rooftops, beyond the River Esk to the West Cliff of Whitby...the New Side. It was a splendid view with the huge, white Royal Hotel dominating the skyline. Next to it, the Whale Bone Arch and Captain Cook’s Statue, both silhouetted against the blue.

“Bet this is for coffin-carriers to have a rest on their way up to the grave-yard!” panted Jamie. “Thank goodness we’ve only got to get to step *Ninety-Nine*!”

They carried on...and less than a minute later they both stopped and looked at one another. The ninety-ninth step had been reached.

It was just a little lower down the staircase than another black lamp-post on the right.

But, much to their disappointment, there was no sign of a door!

Just footworn solid slabs of paving stone lay beneath their feet.

Jessica looked over the iron railings down to the cobbles of Donkey Road.

“Perhaps it’s down there somewhere!” she suggested.

Jamie was staring up at the lamp-post...the old fashioned sort with a four sided lantern above a couple of chubby ladder-rest arms.

“I wonder why just one of the faces of the lantern has red glass and the others are plain?”

“Well,” thought Jessica, “judging by the direction the red’s facing...out to sea...I reckon it’s to guide ships into the harbour at night when the lamp’s shining. As they’re sailing towards Whitby, I bet they line it up with the big red light at the end of the pier out there!”

"Clever stuff, sis! You're not as daft as you loo..!"
"And she is quite correct, Sir!" came a sudden, deep voice from behind.
"Well done, young lady, you have hit the nail completely on the head!"
The tall, angular man was dressed as *Count Dracula* and was leading a group of brightly clad holiday-makers and black Goths. There must have been about twenty of them trailing down the steps behind him.
"If you would care to join my party," the deep voice continued, "I will show you around the church and the Abbey... at no cost! Your knowledge may be valuable!"
Then his voice dropped, and he whispered to Jessica,
"You see, I'm rather new at this game...guiding the tourists!"
"Well, I must say that you certainly *look* the part!" beamed Jessica.
"I think your outfit is fantastic!!"
Count Dracula's jet black hair was swept back and plastered flat against his skull. It shone in the afternoon Sun. His face was chalky white with brilliant blood-shot eyes, fierce eye-brows and convincing fangs.
He was wearing a long, shimmering, high-collared, black cloak and long black boots with silver buckles and pointed toes. One of his bejewelled hands clutched a slender black cane with a silver handle. The other he held in front of his scarlet waistcoat...a peculiar stuffed bat, with outstretched wings, perched on his thumb.
"I'm afraid my sister and I are on a top-secret mission!" chirped Jamie, amazingly politely. "We'd love to join your group...but we've got things to do!"
With that, the man smiled, raised his eye-brows and bowed.
"So be it!" his deep voice rumbled. "Enjoy the rest of the day, and I wish you good fortune with your mission to find your fa...!"
He stopped suddenly, as though he'd said too much.

He began to climb the steps with his followers behind.
"I may see you this evening...on my *Ghost Walk*!" he called back. "Or perhaps during the firework display!!"

Moments later, he and his party had merged into the throng of tourists pouring up and down the steps. Jessica and Jamie looked at one another, curiosity scrawled across their faces.
"That was all a bit peculiar!" said Jessica. "Especially when he wished us good luck with our mission...!"
"And then he stopped so sharply!" agreed Jamie. "I reckon there was something strange about him, and you know what? There was something about him that seemed..."
"Familiar?" finished Jessica, leaning over the railings and gazing down at Donkey Road.
Jamie nodded.
"Yes, that's it!" he said. "I'm sure I've met that guy somewhere else! There's something about him I recognize, but I can't quite put my finger...!"
"Jamie! Look down there!" Jessica suddenly exclaimed, pointing directly beneath them.
They both stared down at the almost deserted, steeply cobbled lane, their mouths wide open with astonishment!

For there...drawn in chalk, across several flat cobbles, were three white spiral patterns...as clear as daylight...just like ammonites!
"They weren't there a couple of minutes ago!!" gasped Jessica.
"They've been drawn while that guy was talking to us!"
There was no holding them back!
Instantly they pelted down the steps as quickly as they could, weaving in and out of the torrent of tourists. At the bottom of the staircase, they turned sharp left and dashed up Donkey Road.
Panting and spluttering...
...they reached the cobbles directly beneath the ninety-ninth step and the black lamp-post with the red glass...
...their eyes darted everywhere, trying to spot the three white spirals...

...but they were nowhere to be found...
...they'd vanished...dissolved away!

But the children *knew* that the spirals had been a clue... a magical signpost...for their eyes only!
And all they could do now...
...was...watch...
...and wait!!

Chapter 15

For the rest of the afternoon, as the Sun slowly dipped in the west and shadows lengthened, Jessica and Jamie hung around Donkey Road, venturing no further away than the bottom of the *One-Hundred and Ninety-Nine Steps*. Constantly they glanced at the cobbles and the great wall beneath the ninety-ninth step, wishing that something...*any*thing...would happen!

Would there be another magical sign?
Something completely unexpected?
Would the drawer of the white spirals appear?

They waited and watched.
They watched and waited.
But nothing happened.

As darkness fell, the cascade of tourists and holiday-makers that tumbled up and down the famous staircase began to slowly dry up. The continuous pitter-pattter of footsteps and the chattering of counting children slowly began to lessen. Soon, as though a tap had

been turned off, the ancient cobbles and paving stones were deserted.
The quaint, little shops in Church Street closed.
Their lights went out and the shopkeepers locked up and went home.
And, slowly but surely, a silence descended on that part of Old Whitby.
A silence that had fallen every night for year upon year...for centuries...
back into the mists of time.
The sky was still clear but now it was jet black rather than soft blue.
Stars were just beginning to be scattered across it like diamond dust
across black velvet.
And the Full Moon was rising once again.
Jessica and Jamie watched and waited.
They waited and watched.
Nothing.
And it was becoming chillier...and chillier.

And then...just moments after the bells of St. Mary's had struck eight o'clock, Jessica nudged Jamie sharply with her elbow.
They were huddled together, just beginning to shiver, leaning on the high stone wall that held up the famous steps.
"Did you hear *that*?" she whispered.
Jamie shook his head.
"There...there it goes again!"
Then they both heard it.

A faint rumbling...a grating, grinding of stone upon stone!
Without another word, Jessica pointed at the mossy, lichen covered wall, just a little further up Donkey Road from where they were standing...where the stones in the wall suddenly became much larger, just before a drain nestled in the cobbles...directly beneath the lamp-post on the staircase with its red face now shining out to sea.
The two children stared in astonishment...as one of the first great stones...in the third or fourth layer up from the road...slowly began to

move to the side...allowing a dribble of warm orange light to lap gently across the cobbles from a widening gap between the moving stone and its motionless neighbour.
On and on the stone slid until the gap was nearly as wide as the stone was high. Then it stopped. All was quiet. The orange light had turned from a dribble into a flood and washed across the whole width of Donkey Road, enticing Jessica and Jamie towards its warm welcome. Slowly they crept up to the large alluring cavity, both of them half-expecting a smiling face to suddenly appear or a beckoning hand to tempt them in!
Closer and closer they crept, until they could peer into the brilliant orange which totally filled a rough, stone tunnel through the thickness of the wall.
"Come on!!" whispered Jessica. "This must be *Golphin's Door*...we've *got* to crawl through! Agreed?"
Jamie nodded, as his sister clambered into the hole and started pulling herself head first along the tight, rocky passageway. There was just enough room to squeeze through.

"There's a cellar with piles of barrels!" she whispered excitedly. "And I can see an archway in the far wall...and a lamp-post! I can't believe it!"
Before he followed his sister, Jamie cast a quick glance down the silvery Donkey Road to check that there was no one watching.
All seemed quiet and still...but then he spotted movement near the bottom of the steps. A familiar face had suddenly appeared, poking around the corner near *Spindle Top* cottage. It was the unmistakable face of *Count Dracula*, the tourist-guide, now looking much more sinister and menacing in the moonlight than he had been during the day! He was leading his evening *Ghost Walk.*
"Follow me, ladies and gentlemen," the deep voice echoed across the cobbles, "and I'll tell you the story of '*The Ghost of the Church Steps*'! Gather round!"

Quickly, Jamie scurried into the hole in the wall, turned around inside and glanced down the road. His eyes met *Count Dracula's* blood-shot eyes just before his party crowded around him. The *Count* smiled an eerie smile, his white fangs glinting in the moonlight. But, somehow, once again, it was a smile that Jamie *knew*...although he couldn't work out how or why! He was absolutely certain that he'd seen the face before! And strangely, the smile seemed to be one of approval. It was as though the *Count* seemed to know exactly where Jessica and Jamie were going!

As the tourists gathered around the guide, Jamie sank further into the passageway...and the stone-slab began to close, with the same grating and grinding as before. The orange tide of light on the cobbles ebbed away and then vanished as the gap became narrower and narrower...until the stone door shut fast with a final, dull thud.
The children had, well and truly, been swallowed!
But, *who* or *what* had opened and closed the door?
What would they find in the dark, dank underworld, deep beneath Old Whitby?
Would they find their father?
Would they ever see the light of day again?
And...just *who* was under that *Count Dracula* disguise?

The cellar was large and square with a low ceiling.
Its walls were mostly roughly cut out of the sandstone, but there were one or two sections which were made of carved, rectangular stones, similar to the ones that made the wall outside...on Donkey Road...but without the same mossy and lichen patches. There were lots of eerie nooks and crannies where the light didn't reach, but, on the whole, the orange light cast by the lamp warmly illuminated the room and its piles of barrels.
The air was also strangely warm, much warmer than outside. It almost had a damp, humid feel about it...so much so, that beads of sweat glistened on the foreheads of the two children.
Jessica sniffed the air.
She could sense woodsmoke mixed with the familiar smell of sea, shingle and sea-weed.
"It's so quiet," she whispered, softer than she had ever whispered before,

while her eyes explored the strange room. “I wonder when the last person stood where we’re standing! Could have been centur...!”
“Cor! Look at at this lot!” suddenly exclaimed Jamie in just about the loudest whisper possible!
He had removed the circular, wooden lids from a couple of the barrels.

“There was I, thinking they might be loaded with gunpowder!” he beamed. “And instead they’re full to the brim with hundreds of tiny swords, cutlasses and those broad, curved ones!”
“Scimitars!” whispered Jessica, marvelling at the fantastic hoard of twinkling treasure. “Scimitars from ancient Turkey and Persia!”
It was, indeed, an amazing sight!
Every single weapon was shining brightly, without even a hint of tarnish or rust! And they were all just crammed into the barrels, pointing in every direction. But it was the size of each blade of glinting metal that surprised the children the most...they were all only about the length of half a pencil!
From the mass of silvery-bronze, she carefully picked a slender sword with a ruby encrusted hilt and placed it across the palm of her other hand.
“It’s so light!” she gasped. “It’s so beautiful! Just look at the carved detail and those jewels! It’s like a small paper-knife!”

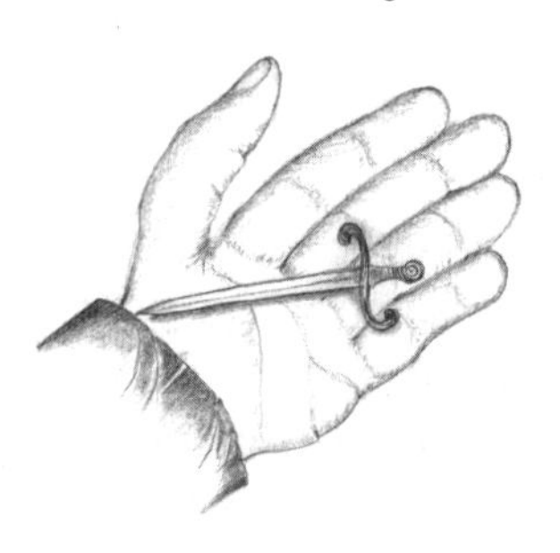

But Jamie had already plunged into the miniature armoury and was having a playful duel between his left hand and his right!
The pirate’s cutlass in his right hand was definitely overpowering the slim rapier in his left, the sound of sharp, scraping, slashing steel echoing around the cellar.
“Sshh!” whispered Jessica, impatiently grabbing hold of Jamie’s animated elbows.
“We don’t want to be heard!”
“But there isn’t a single soul in here!” grumbled Jamie, his blades coming to a reluctant standstill.
“We don’t know who’s through that archway!” warned Jessica, carefully

returning her sword and eying the lamp-post.
"Let's have a look in another barrel!" insisted Jamie, excitedly.
They opened one each...and their jaws dropped as they gazed at their contents!
One was absolutely full of spears...each long, wooden shaft tipped with a vicious, metal point...all jammed in their barrel, tips down, like dozens and dozens and dozens of giant toothpicks!
And the other was crammed with miniature long-bows and cross-bows, all tightly strung for action and accompanied by a higgledy-piggledy mass of silver quivers all stuffed with feathered arrows and bolts!
"If every single barrel here is full of weapons...," Jamie considered, "then there must be enough for an army of *thousands*!!"
"Come on!" beckoned Jessica, anxious to explore beyond the lamp-post. "Follow me, and keep your eyes peeled!"

They tip-toed across the sandy floor, closer and closer to the rough cut archway. As they approached it, they could feel on their cheeks a gentle, warm breeze which carried the peculiar scent of woodsmoke mixed with brine and seaweed. But even more peculiar was the archway itself! When they'd looked at it from across the cellar it had seemed much higher than they were tall! Perhaps that was something to do with the height of the lamp-post! An optical illusion. But now that they'd actually reached it, they had to stoop forward otherwise they would bang their heads! And the lamp-post...just beyond the rocky mouth...was only about as tall as Jamie, or up to Jessica's chest!
They leaned on the left-hand side of the archway and looked at one another, wondering what was coming next, their heartbeats pounding in their chests, throats and ears!
Nervously, they peeped around the corner...

...and what they saw...

...made their heads instantly spring back!

They stared at each other in total, shocked surprise!
They'd set their eyes on some weird and wonderful sights during the last year or so...but *this* definitely took the biscuit!!
"Wowee!!" gasped Jessica, her eyes almost flickering in the orange light of the lamp-post. "Just look at *that*!!"

Chapter 16

Before them was an amazing subterranean street! In every detail just like one you would have found in any town in England, maybe one hundred and fifty, or two hundred years ago...but magnificently smaller...like a cross between a model town and a real one! Red tiled roofs marched in both directions down both sides of a slightly curved and sloping cobbled road with no pavements. Glowing, orange lit lamp-posts were evenly spaced in front of the buildings, illuminating the dozens of bottle-glassed bay windows of shops and houses. Painted signs noiselessly swung in the breeze, denoting tobacconists, fish-mongers, candle-makers, rope-makers, lock-smiths, jewellers, butchers, bakers...

But the whole place was utterly deserted and devoid of a single person or animal...yet it all had a freshness and vitality that suggested that the street had only recently been abandoned. Even smoke wound lazily upwards from a host of little chimney pots towards the vast, over-arching, soot covered cavern roof.

Almost shyly, the children crept into the street, in awe of the hidden, secret world into which they had stumbled. A world completely unknown to the busy, twenty-first century Whitby which was just steps...yet centuries...away! Surely such a place couldn't be full of the hustle and bustle of street life at the very same time as the hustle and bustle of present-day Whitby. Surely they couldn't exist unknown to one

another, just separated by a stone's throw!
It really seemed as though the children had literally stepped back in time, into a world that was going about *its* everyday life at the very same moment in time as the world outside was going about *its* everyday life!
Surely this couldn't be another *Aqua Crysta*?
Another secret world apart from the rest?
Perhaps that was why the street lay abandoned!
Intruders from the future world had entered the cellar!
Panic had set in!
The people had fled!
Pangs of guilt flashed through the minds of both travellers!
Were they doing the right thing?
Should they re-trace their steps?
Leave the place in peace, and say nothing to anyone...just like they'd done with their discovery of *Aqua Crysta*!
It was at that moment of doubt that they had a reminder...a reminder of why they were there!
Jessica saw them first.
Three of them, carved into a stone archway that spanned the street, just a few houses down the slope to the left.
Three gilted ammonites.
She pointed them out to Jamie, and they both knew that they had to carry on!

It seemed so strange to be walking down a street where the upstairs windows were level with their eyes. They felt like giants. In *Aqua Crysta* they always shrank into the surroundings and almost felt at home, but here they felt totally clumsy and out of place!
They imagined a person, if they ever saw one, would be about knee-high to them, or a bit taller. That was confirmed by the height of the doors and the length of the beds in the upstairs rooms. Looking into the bedrooms reminded Jessica of the dolls' house in the *Forest Cellar*, but, of course, all the furniture here was twice, or even three times the size.
When they reached the stone archway with the ammonites they had to

crawl through it on hands and knees, being careful not to get stuck! Afterwards the street began to dip more steeply.
The strangest thing was that all the food in the shops seemed to be fresh and new. The vegetables and fruit seemed to have just been picked! Jamie, of course, couldn't resist bending down and helping himself to a carrot and an apple from a couple of sacks in front of a grocer's shop. The carrot was no longer than a paper-clip and the apple no bigger than a marble, but both were crunchy and juicy.
"It's funny that back home in *Aqua Crysta*, all the grub is huge!" he mumbled as he licked his lips. "Gi-normous blackberries and acorns from the Upper World...but here, everything is tiny!"
"Not like *your* appetite then!" grumbled Jessica. "Can't you, for once, just stop eating! You need to go on a diet!"
"I'm already on a diet!" beamed Jamie, helping himself to another shiny, red apple. "A *sea-food* diet! I *see food*, and I eat it! Get it?"
Jessica shook her head, tutted, and raised her eyes in disapproval to the cavern roof.
Instantly, she was amazed by the sheer size of the vast cave that seemed to envelop the street and its smaller, narrower side alleys. It was like a huge umbrella, thickly blackened by all the smoke from the countless chimneys.
"To think that Whitby Abbey and St. Mary's Church are somewhere above that lot!" she gasped in wonder.

A couple of minutes later they came to a group of shops with trapdoors gaping wide open in front of them. Each one was about the size of a large table-mat. Ladders or steps led down into them...and for some unknown reason, a peculiar, flickering, bright yellowy-red light beamed out of each.

Jamie tried to peer into one but was driven back by the heat.
"It's so bright and hot down there, I can't make out *anything*!" he grumbled, his face glistening with beads of sweat even more than ever.

"Well, at least we're on the right track!" said Jessica, pointing to a set of three ammonites above a lock-smith's door.

Shortly afterwards, the main street dipped even steeper and the cobbles stopped. Now the houses were just on the left-hand side and a wide flight of steps plunged into the unknown. Smoke still poured from all the chimneys, yet the air still smelled quite pleasant, aided by a strengthening sea-breeze. The houses here seemed much slimmer, taller and more elegant than earlier and had a black and white Tudor feel about them, although the roof tiles were still red. And instead of large panes of glass in their windows, or bottle-glass, they all seemed to have delicate, diamond patterns.
There were no more street lamps and the only light came from burning candles and blazing fires in the hearths. Opposite the houses were the rough, jagged rocks of the cavern, and heaps of quarried crystal which had a faint, milky-white glow about them.
"The houses seem to be just that bit bigger here, don't you think?" said Jessica, as she leapt down the steps, three or four at a time.
"But they all look as though the folk who live in them have just vanished!" replied Jamie, nodding his head. "Every house has got a fire, and there's piles of wood next to each fireplace, all ready to be chucked on!"

Suddenly, Jessica stopped, nearly causing Jamie to plough straight into her. She pointed to another trio of ammonites set into a house wall.
"It must mean that we're still on the right track!" she beamed with a re-assured smile. "I'm sure Dad and *Deer Leap*'ll be down here somewhere!"
"It's like following one his treasure-trails through the Forest or back in Scotland!" said Jamie.
Gradually, the slope eased off and cottages and houses became even larger...so much so that their front doors looked the normal size!

Thousands of blackened stalactites clung to the cavern roof, and small ones, like icicles, even dripped from the windowsills and roofs.
Fat, squat stalagmites sprung from the gritty floor, and some of the cottage roofs even had hardened, flows of rock smothering their red tiles.
"I reckon these are the oldest houses we've seen!" suggested Jessica.
"It's as though the further we go down, the older the buildings...!"
"And the bigger they are!" burst Jamie, suddenly pointing to one particular cottage with a familiar set of ammonites above its front door.
"And have you noticed that the houses here have *no glass at all* in their windows!" said Jessica.
It was true. The cottages down here seemed rougher and simpler than all the others they'd seen.
"Come on!" urged Jamie. "Let's have a look inside and have a rest for a few minutes! We seem to have been on the move for hours!!"
Jessica stood on the worn stone step and peered through a little diamond shaped hole in the front door. Jamie gently pushed on the round door-knob. Slowly, the rough, wooden door swung inwards with just the slightest of creaks and the children stared into the gloomy downstairs room.

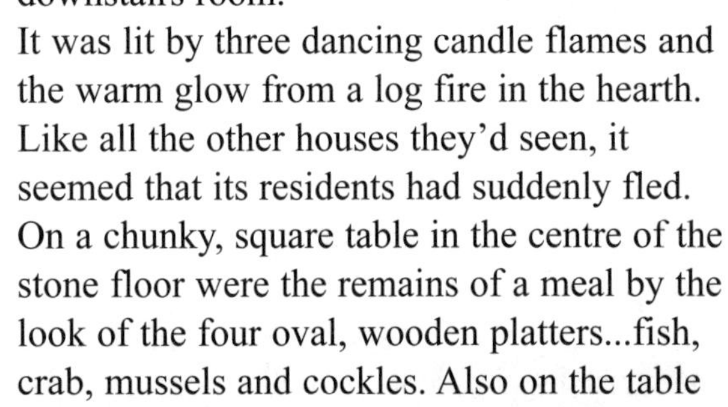

It was lit by three dancing candle flames and the warm glow from a log fire in the hearth. Like all the other houses they'd seen, it seemed that its residents had suddenly fled.
On a chunky, square table in the centre of the stone floor were the remains of a meal by the look of the four oval, wooden platters...fish, crab, mussels and cockles. Also on the table was half a cob of white bread and four, nearly full, wooden drinking goblets. In the middle, next to the three candles, sat a matching flagon of black, frothy liquid...beer, according to Jamie's nose! It seemed that four people had been eating and drinking when they had been inconveniently disturbed!
The rest of the furniture in the room was plain and simple. The only chairs were the four around the table. There were a couple of large chests in one particularly dark corner, both draped in drab coloured

clothes and the bareness of the walls was only broken by a few uncluttered shelves and three small, glassless windows. Beneath one window was a wooden pail, about the size and shape of half a barrel, plus several smaller ones. Scattered in the hearth was a tangle of cooking pots of various sizes.
A ladder led up through a square hole in the low ceiling into the even gloomier upper room.
"It reminds me of *Old Soulsyke*!" whispered Jessica, wondering whether or not to have a peep upstairs. "Especially this ladd...!"
Suddenly, the front door banged to! The explosion inside the cottage was so loud it could have woken the dead! Everything seemed to shake, including the children!!
Jessica and Jamie looked at one another with shock mixed with fear across their faces!
"The breeze must have caught it!" whispered Jessica, with a tremble in her voice. "Come on, let's get going! The noise might attract someone!"
She grabbed hold of the door-knob and pulled.
The door wouldn't move.
It seemed jammed.
"Curse! It's stuck!" she exclaimed.
"Let me have a go!"
Jamie pulled for all he was worth, but *still*, the door wouldn't budge!

And then...they heard it!!

A faint, cackling laughter coming from the other side of the door!
A menacing, evil laughter!
Jessica nervously plucked up the courage and slowly moved her head towards the little diamond shaped hole in the door.
Dreading what she would set her eyes upon, she peered into the darkness beyond...
...and what she saw...made her gasp with horror...!!

Chapter 17

An almost straight, straining chain of knee-high people stretched from the other side of the door across the cavern floor to the distant dark wall. There must have been a hundred of them or more, all heaving on a rope which had been quickly hooked and knotted around the door-knob. Most of their faces were contorted and twisted by the effort they were exerting, while others were laughing and gasping for breath. Besides the heaving line were more diminutive people, mostly women-folk, urging the men to pull harder and harder on the rope!
It was like some enormous tug-of-war with the small cottage as the solid, unmovable opposition!
Then one of the older women, with long, straggly white hair, stood on the door-step and rapped on the door with her fist.
"We have you trapped!" she screamed in a witch-like cackle. "There is *no* escape and *The Golphin* will be pleased with our catch, this fine morning!"
Jessica and Jamie were absolutely speechless! And terrified!
They had been well and truly caught by surprise! Everything had been going so smoothly...that they had completely forgotten about the dangers that could strike at any moment! And now, when they least expected it, they had been ambushed and trapped like mice in a bottle-trap!
Jamie anxiously peeped through one of the window holes and looked at the horde of dwarf-like people.

"If we can crawl through one of the windows and make a run for it!" he whispered. "I'm sure we can out-run them...they're tiny!"
"And where do we run *to*?" replied Jessica, still gazing at the horrifying sight outside the cottage. "Further down into the unknown? Or up to the Victorian street and hope we can somehow open the stone door?"
Suddenly, the windows were covered with what looked like layers and layers of tangled, knotted fishing nets, made worse by dozens of wizened, shrivelled, wrinkled faces peering through the gaps accompanied by waving bony arms and pointing long-nailed fingers. Any hope of escape had vanished, and the cackling and screaming was becoming more and more feverish and frenzied!
Jessica grabbed hold of Jamie by the shoulders and looked him straight in the eyes.
"Now look," she said grimly, "there's only one way out of this! We've got to talk to them, calm them down. I don't think they want to harm us. Perhaps they're quite peaceful folk normally. It's just that we've invaded their world...!"
"Sis, all I can say is that they don't *look* very peaceful!" burst Jamie, glancing at the mayhem outside the cottage. "In fact I reckon they're becoming more and more angry and hysterical by the second! I think they want our blood!"
"They remind me of the folk who lived under *Needle Crag*!" said Jessica as calmly as she could. "Remember? Hester and Gwenda...?"
"More like *Grizel*, that nasty piece of work!" replied Jamie, recalling the dwarf who tried to poison them.
"They're all about the same size, too!" Jessica carried on. "Something to do with the shrinking power of those *Crystals of Eternity*! Perhaps there was a community of normal-sized people here once and they've gradually become smaller and smaller over the centuries! Like at *Needle Crag* where Mayor Merrick's twin sisters lived!"
Jessica paused, glanced through the diamond shaped hole in the door and then looked back at her brother.
"Look, I've definitely decided!" she said. "We're going to *talk* to them!"
"But how are you going to stop that din?" shouted Jamie.
"Just watch this...and learn!" said Jessica, with the beginnings of a

nervous grin breaking out across her face, although she was inwardly terrified.
First, she rolled up her anorak sleeve on her right arm and then the sleeve of her pullover.
"Ready?" she called above the racket outside.
Jamie nodded, wondering what on earth his sister was up to, but, at the same time, quietly admiring it all!
Then, with a great flourish, she poked her arm out of the diamond shaped hole and started waving it as vigorously as she could!
The effect was immediate and almost magical!
In an instant, the noise stopped dead...as though a switch had been turned off! There wasn't a single sound!
Somehow, the gesture had been viewed as a sign of friendship.
Jessica and Jamie were not a pair of vicious animals who could bite or even kill. They had come in peace and meant no harm at all!
Jessica carried on waving madly...and amazingly, the tug-of-war rope slackened and the fishing-nets began to be removed from the windows.
"Ready for the next step?" she whispered to her awe-struck brother.
Jamie nodded, as he gazed and tried to smile at the puzzled, ancient faces staring at him through the window.
"Ready when you are!" he whispered back through the side of his mouth.
Jessica slowly withdrew her arm and then pulled on the door-knob...
...and, this time, the door swung open with the same slight creak as before.
The horde of people gasped and sighed as they set eyes on one of the children they had trapped, framed in the doorway.
She seemed like a giant!
"Jamie, come and stand by me!" she whispered.
Jamie gulped and nervously shuffled over to his sister.
Then, when he appeared in the doorway, another wave of gasps and sighs swept over the crowd.
Somehow, their hysteria had been quelled.
Jamie admiringly glanced up at his sister.
"Wow, Sis! You've done it!" he whispered.
"Now comes the tricky bit!" Jessica replied. "Just keep your fingers crossed!"

She looked at the tiny, witchy woman who had rapped on the door with her fist, smiled, bent down slowly and held out a hand of friendship.
The woman, dressed in a long, drab brown dress, with leather booted feet, looked up at Jessica with a hint of a twinkle in her small brown eyes set like little pebbles in her pale, gaunt, hollow-cheeked face.
"Hello!" said Jessica boldly. "My name is Jessica and this is my younger brother, Jamie. We have travelled from the Magical Realm of Queen Venetia, the Land known as *Aqua Crysta*. We have come in search of our father!"
Another gasp filled the cavern.
The white haired woman raised her small hand, which was no larger than that of a doll, and gently touched Jessica's enormous finger tips.
"Greetings! I am Lady Celestine, Eldest of the Saltwicks!"
Her voice now was gentle and quiet, nothing like the harsh outburst she had cackled and screamed earlier.
"Your face seems somehow familiar!" she went on, her countrymen and women gradually deserting the rope and the nets and crowding inquisitively around the cottage. "I wonder if your father could be the Man in the Bay...the giant that was magicked to our small Kingdom months ago. The Giant Man the *Grykes* have chained to the ruined beach house there! Bend down further, my dear, let me look at your face!"
Jessica bent down and allowed Lady Celestine to look into her deep blue eyes, that were the image of her father's.
The Eldest of the Saltwicks smiled.
"You are indeed his daughter! I will take you to him, but be warned, there will be many perils ahead. The *Grykes* prize your father greatly, and mean to do evil business with him. He is being held hostage in the magic and the payment for his release will be mighty. The *Grykes* are an unconquerable force, but when they are in league with the *Shym-ryn* from the moors and woodlands...*nothing* can stop them! We have been under their iron thumbs for many centuries! Resistance is useless!"

So, with the wonderful news that their father was at least safe and wasn't too far away, a rather remarkable procession marched down past more simple, but full-sized cottages heading towards the sea. As the briny breeze gradually became stronger and fresher, the two children, hardly believing what was happening to them, were followed by a dancing, singing throng of hundreds of knee-high, happy Saltwicks! It was an incredible scene! Jessica and Jamie almost felt like a pair of Pied Pipers!

Apparently, according to snippets of chatter they heard from Lady Celestine and her companions, the Saltwicks (actually pronounced '*Salt-icks*') had lived in caves just to the south of Whitby for centuries, living off the fruits of the North Sea and what they could raid from Whitby ships. But as they had gradually shrunk in stature over many generations, they had cut themselves off from Whitby folk and built smaller and smaller houses further and further up and into the steep floored caverns. Their most recent houses being in the Victorian streets and alleyways, just beneath the Abbey Steps, next to the cellar with the barrels. Many Saltwicks lived up there, but most lived in houses and cottages that were far too large for them, but at least they were near their beloved Bay!

"But where do the dreaded *Grykes* live?" asked Jamie, as he sat down for a rest on a rock overlooking the rooftops of Saltwick village, the cavern mouth and the sea and the bright blue sky beyond. Daylight flooded into the cavern and lit the red roofs of scores of cottages.

"See the steps on the other side of the stream?" replied Lady Celestine. "Follow them and you will come to a towering, arched door. Through that is the devilish World of the *Grykes*! It is said that their Land stretches beneath the sea. There are thousands and thousands of them and each one is no taller than the length of your foot! Less than half *my* size! They are ruled by the iron grip of *The Golphin*! He controls them like a queen ant controls her workers and soldiers. They move quickly and fearlessly in great columns, clad in silver armour from head to toe. They are the fiercest of

all Goblins and follow every order from their leader to the death!"
"Have you ever met *The Golphin*?" asked Jessica.
"No, but I believe he is much larger than his troops and wears a golden helmet of invincibility in the shape of a pair of ammonites! It is said that he never removes it! And if he does he will die!"
"What about the *Grykes*?" wondered Jamie. "Do you have much to do with them?"
"Only when their giant door opens and they pour through our modest Kingdom pillaging and plundering for food and precious stones and crystals! Just one small colony live up in the cellar near our Victorian street! They spy on us and see that we don't get up to any mischief!"
"You mean when we crawled through the stone door into the cellar from the Abbey Steps, they were *watching* us?" Jessica exclaimed.
Lady Celestine nodded her head.
"Yes, and it is they who will have opened the door for you...and closed it! They are small and thin, and hide easily in nooks and crannies! In fact the word '*gryke*' actually means '*crack in the rock*'!"

Soon afterwards, most of the Saltwicks had either vanished into their out-sized homes or had climbed the steps to the Tudor black and white houses or beyond to the more comfortable Victorian street and alleyways.
Lady Celestine led the children down to a stone bridge over the stream and pointed to the vast mouth of the cavern.
"I must leave you here and wish you good fortune!" she said. "As I said, your father is chained to a ruined beach cottage on the rocks of Saltwick Bay, just outside the cavern to the right. He will be happy to see you, I am sure. You will see a basket full of seafood we have collected. Take it to him. We have fed him every day since he was magicked there! By order of *The Golphin*, of course! I hope you find your father well and in good spirits, although you must remember he has had a hard time...a *very hard* time, indeed!"

With that, the Lady swept away and left the children to wander down the stream's shingle bank towards the sea, past piles of cockle and mussel shells, drying fishing-nets, drifts of smelly sea-weed and small

rowing boats. At the mouth of the cave they passed a giant anchor and a pile of polished ammonites. Once on the open sandy seashore, they turned right and headed along the beach of a wide curved bay...Saltwick Bay.
A great rocky headland bounded the bay at the far end and just before it they could make out a small cottage with a curl of black smoke winding up into the blue sky.
"Do you think he's *really* there?" asked Jamie, as he scooped up a handful of sand and breathed in the fresh salty air, the briny breeze tugging at his ginger hair.

Suddenly, Jessica stopped dead in her tracks!
She stared into Jamie's eyes with a sudden look of fear.
"Hang on a minute!" she said quietly, with a quiver in her voice. "There's something funny going on here! When we crawled into the cellar it was night time. Right? It was dark in Whitby. Yes?"
Jamie nodded.
"Well how come it's now a bright, sunny day? We haven't been underground *that lon...!*"
It was at that moment both of them noticed a glint of reflected sunlight coming from the cavern mouth behind them.
Then another glint...and another!
And then hundreds of glints!
A whole mass of moving, shining silver had suddenly crept from the mouth of the cavern!
A whole army!
A tide of tiny Goblins!
Marching towards them!

The dreaded *Grykes* had followed them out onto the beach...
...and now, they meant business!!

Chapter 18

The silver tide of countless, angry looking Goblins swept around the children like sea-water flowing around a sandcastle on the beach. It was as though they acted as one huge, flowing creature, almost like volcanic lava streaming from the cavern's mouth.
Their tiny faces were angular and harsh, with long pointed noses, ears and chins. Their mouths wide and snarling, beneath small eyes crowned with bushy, brown eyebrows. But it was their silveriness that was most striking in the unexpected sunshine. They were all clad identically in gleaming armour from head to toe, making even their faces seem metallic...each and every individual grasping either a silver sword, bow or spear...just the same weapons Jessica and Jamie had discovered in the barrels in the cellar beneath the Abbey Steps. And, even more strangely, as the silver tide crept closer and closer to the children's giant, fluorescent trainers, there was hardly a sound, other than the constant, dull thud of hundreds of silvered boots treading across the soft sand...all in exact step with one another, as if they were the feet of one, single, enormous, disciplined creature.
Jessica and Jamie had frozen like statues, unable to move in any direction. By now the broad, wide flood of *Grykes* had completely surrounded them. There was no escape.
It was then that they noticed a solitary, knee-high figure had appeared in

the cavern mouth...Lady Celestine, a guilty smirk about her thin lips. Jessica was furious.
"You told them!" she yelled.
The Lady nodded.
"I had to, for the sake of my people! We have to favour our masters whenever we can, otherwise they will treat us even more cruelly...!"
"And now my brother and I are trapped, at their mercy, thanks to you!"
"They will not harm you. You are too valuable...along with your father! You will be used in some bargain or other...the nature of which I do not know. *The Golphin* will see to that! But for now...you are safe!"
Jessica and Jamie looked anxiously at the solid, swarm of soldier Goblins surrounding them.
It certainly didn't *seem* safe!
And the *Grykes* didn't exactly *seem* harm...!
Then suddenly, to the complete surprise of everyone, an explosion rang out from beyond the cavern mouth!
The Goblins, as one, turned to look in the direction of the seaweed, strewn rocks towards Whitby...as did the trapped children and Lady Celestine.
Another explosion rang out!
Then another!
Lead shot hit the black, shale cliffs sending clouds of dust and fragments of rock into the air and over the silver army.
The explosions had been *gunfire*!
Then, from behind the seaweed covered rocks...six, seven, eight figures appeared...normal sized, bearded men, dressed in black and white striped vests and baggy blue trousers, two of them waving old-fashioned, long-barrelled muskets. The others were scrambling over the rocks, picking up pebbles and hurling them at the swarm of Goblins.
At first, the obedient, fearless horde of soldier *Grykes* held their ground and formation, but then as the pebbles and lead-shot began to rain down on them, they dissolved into confusion, abandoned their captives and shrank back into the cavern. One or two spears were hurled at their attackers, but within a few seconds the whole, ferocious throng of Goblins had been reduced to an almost cowardly rabble, retreating up the steps towards their door and their secret underworld and, no doubt,

to the wrath of *The Golphin*!
As the vast army melted away, Jessica and Jamie noticed the one and only casualty from the skirmish.
Dead, at the cavern mouth, a slender, silver spear piercing her ragged body...Lady Celestine...killed in angry vengeance by the *Grykes*.
She had paid the highest price for her treachery towards Jessica and Jamie!

A moment later, the cheering, bearded rescuers rushed across the sands to be met with beaming smiles from Jessica and Jamie.
But before the children could utter a single word of thanks, they were both, totally unexpectedly, flung headlong into another, instant nightmare! For instead of being able to thank the men and explain that they were trying to reach their father in the cottage at the end of the beach...they were roughly grabbed, their hands bound by thick, coarse rope and their mouths silenced by greasy cloth gags! And, despite their futile struggles, the children were led in grips of iron, over the slippery, seaweed-strewn rocks towards Whitby!
They could hardly believe what was happening to them!
First, they'd been surrounded and captured by one enemy!
Then they'd been rescued...and immediately captured by another!
What was happening?
How come these burly men from Whitby, during the October half-term holiday, were treating them like captured criminals!
Were they young thugs...playing some kind of nasty, wicked game?
Why had they got old-fashioned musket guns?
Why was the Sun shining in a blue sky, when it should have been night-time?
How could they get back to the Saltwick beach and their father?
Questions, questions and more questions flashed through the fearful minds of the children as they were almost dragged across the rocks.

But then...as their terrified eyes caught sight of the distant Whitby...
...even more horrifying thoughts filled their heads!
Something wasn't right!
Something was wrong!

This wasn’t the Whitby they had left just hours earlier!
It seemed completely different!
Only half there!

Was it Whitby?
Or were they being dragged to *somewhere else*?

Strange smells began to fill their noses...
...and stranger and stranger sights filled their eyes!

Where on earth *were* they?

Chapter 19

As more and more of Whitby came into view, the stranger it all seemed to be! In between watching where they put their feet on the slippery rocks, and trying to avoid hidden rock pools, the children glanced at the peculiar sights before them, as well as listening to the shouted, harsh words coming from their kidnappers. Jake, their muscular, long haired leader, probably the eldest of the gang, kept on yelling about how a certain ship's captain...a Captain Scraggs...would be 'so chuffed about the catch' and that the 'nippers with the fancy clothes would be worth ten guineas apiece, easy!'

It was the sheer number of sailing ships that struck Jessica and Jamie the most. There seemed to be scores of them...great wooden, three-masted ships, some with huge grubby white and grey sails gently billowing in the warm breeze, some with sails tightly furled.

At least a dozen were anchored out at sea beyond the stone piers and just the *one* lighthouse, while most were hugging the quaysides around the calmer waters of the harbour. In between the giant sailing ships were even more smaller, squatter fishing boats with single or double sails, crews busily emptying bulging nets of fish onto the stone jetties. Mountainous black heaps of coal were dotted amid the fish like giant molehills. Each had men clambering over them, shovelling the coal into huge, wide, flat boats like enormous canal barges with small sails. Across the harbour, the children were shocked to see two gigantic dead whales lying on the dockside ready to be cut up for their meat, blubber oil and bones. And beyond, where the vast, imposing *Royal Hotel* should have been...perched on the cliff top next to Captain Cook's Statue and the Whalebone Arch...there was nothing! Just emptiness! The hotel hadn't even been built yet! It was all so strange, peculiar and dream-like. As though the children had, somehow, travelled back in time...into the past...to Whitby how it used to be...maybe in the early *Nineteenth Century*...the *1830s* or *40s*...before Victorian times!

It all seemed so different!

The whole port seemed to be a breathless, bustling ants' nest of activity, not a leisurely, modern tourist destination. Gone were the cafes and gift shops. Gone were the fish and chips and the candyfloss! Everywhere they looked men were working on the busy quaysides or climbing the mazes of aerial rope rigging. Wooden carts, piled high with cargo and goods, pulled by pairs of horses, rumbled over the cobbles alongside the jumble of ships. Little thatched and red tiled cottages with tiny windows were scattered among the mayhem, next to little workshops and factories with tall chimneys and blazing furnaces pumping smoke into the salty air. Whale oil was bubbling away in huge, iron vats. Long skirted, shawled women in white bonnets sat by baskets and baskets of fish, gutting and boning them like non-stop machines, most of them smoking long, clay tobacco pipes.

Groups of scruffy children were huddled around heaps of mussels, cockles, periwinkles and limpets, shelling them with short, curved knives and tossing the slimy nuggets of flesh into broad-bottomed buckets. Hundreds of filleted herrings dangled from iron bars being cured and preserved above slow-burning piles of wood chippings and sawdust. More women and children were mending great swathes of tangled fishing nets while others were scrubbing and grinding away at little

pieces of jet from the cliffs to be made into jewellery. Stacks of lobster and shrimp pots were everywhere, along with countless coils of rope, wooden barrels of brandy, wine, beer and gunpowder, cages of hens and ducks, churns of milk, piles of stones, bricks and cut timber.

And, strangely...along what should have been Church Street...wandering amid the smoky chaos and the hectic, manic hustle and bustle, were couples of gentile, well dressed ladies and gentlemen attired in similar elegant old-fashioned clothes that Jessica and Jamie had seen in Whitby only hours before! But instead of them being surrounded by throngs of *Twenty-First Century* brightly coloured tourists and sombre, black Goths, they were sailing as gracefully as they could through a sea of hard graft and pungent, salty grime.

On and on, Jessica and Jamie were pushed and pulled through the heaving crowds of Whitby workers, groups of sailors and well-off tourists. Despite their anoraks, jeans and fluorescent trainers, no one even batted an eyelid! They just weren't noticed! And there wasn't a policeman or a friendly face to be seen!

Past the little workshops and cottages, their feet splashed through the mud and the puddles towards the market place and the bridge beyond...not the swing-bridge they had crossed earlier, but a draw-bridge drawn open by tethered horses. Next to the bridge were a couple of inns

fronted by a resting huddle of brightly painted stage-coaches with '*York*' and '*London*' across their doors in fancy gold lettering. More wealthy gentlemen and gentleladies spilled from the inns and casually milled about, drinking wine and brandy, and making polite conversation about the quaintness of *Old Whitby*!

Jessica tried to wave and catch their attention, but it was no use. Jake even threatened to strike her a blow if she didn't co-operate! He made it clear that she and her brother would bring the gang a welcome fortune which they could share and spend on beer and tobacco.

"Stop ya strugglin'!" he snarled from under his black beard. "We'll soon be at yon '*Neptune*' and Cap'n Scraggs'll gi' ye the eye!"

Another of the gang, a pasty-faced, lanky youth with jet black, close-cropped hair and a chin of matching stubble and fiery pimples joked, "And then you'll be cabin nippers, on the Great Briny, livin' on maggots 'n' sea-biscuits!"

Jessica and Jamie looked daggers at their captors and bit deeper into their greasy gags.

This just *could not* be happening!

Please!

Sometime soon, they just *had* to wake up in their snug, little home in Pillo!

Surely!

But no, the nightmare continued as the ships docked beyond the draw-bridge came into view, together with the noise of the busy ship-building yards. The regular beat of hammering and the constant bray of wood-sawing filled the air, even drowning out the never-ending screeching of the gulls.

Only hours before, the children had sat across the same river, on the quiet quayside next to a swing-bridge, nibbling their cakes and sausage-rolls, and looking at the one and only sailing ship, the '*Grand Turk*'!

It seemed like a century ago!

Now, the whole scene was a complete tangle of masts, and sails and rigging!
Dozens of ships, some only half built!
They passed '*Sea Cloud*', '*Orient*' and '*Albatross*'...all fully rigged and ready to sail on the next high tide. Cargoes were being busily loaded onto the graceful vessels as they gently swayed and strained on their mooring ropes. Smart uniformed officers marched along the decks, and brasses and even cannons were being polished by more lowly, striped vested crews.
Then the gang came to the next straining vessel...the smaller, much scruffier ship, the '*Neptune*'.
No fancy polished brasses and lanterns here!
Compared to the rather regal vessels nearer the bridge, it was obvious that the '*Neptune*' had definitely seen better days!

Any paintwork that remained was peeling off, the wood slats of her hull were stained, worn and barnacle-ridden and her sails were dark, grubby grey and threadbare.
A narrow gang-plank connecting her to the quay swayed slightly.
At the top of it stood a severe looking, rotund old man, white wigged and in a scruffy, navy blue uniform of sorts. He was slightly stooping forward in a drunken manner, bloomingly bewhiskered and wearing a black patch over one eye.
Captain Scraggs, presumed the children.
His name and appearance seemed to match his ship!
"Where's ye bin?" he barked at his crew.
"Wait 'n' see what we grabbed on them there rocks b' Saltwick Nab!" Jake shouted back enthusiastically. "Ye wanted cabin-nippers!
We got 'em!"
"Bring 'em aboard! Let me look at 'em!" growled Captain Scraggs,

casting his one good eye on the catch.
"Come on, get a move on! We sail on t' tide in an hour! Take them gags off 'em!"
Jessica and Jamie were shoved up the gang-plank, closer and closer to the evil looking sea-dog who could be their tyrannical master for years to come!
"Strange sort of clobber they're a wearin'!" he snapped as he eyed the children up and down. "Open yer jaws and let me see tha' teeth! We'll see what yer worth!"
Jessica gulped, glanced anxiously at her brother, and gazed at the hideous Cyclops skipper.
She took a deep breath.
"We are *not* for sale!" she burst. "We're looking for our father, and have no intention what-so-ever of going to sea!"
"Here, here!" exploded Jamie, looking at his sister, wondering what on earth she was going to say next!
The captain looked flabber-ghasted.
"We'll see about that!" he barked, his overgrown eyebrows knitting viciously together. "Now keep yer tongues still! Yer speak when I tells ye an' not before! Now open yer jaws! Both o' ye!"
Jessica and Jamie clenched their mouths tightly shut.
There was a short silence, while the captain rubbed his chin and pondered, his eyebrows gradually untangling.
Then came the words the children dreaded.
"I'll take 'em! I like their spirit! I'll soon knock some sense into 'em! How much?"
"Twenty guineas for the big 'un! Fifteen for the red haired 'un!" said Jake.
"Twenty-five for 'em both!" barked Scraggs.
The gang looked at one another.
"Thirty guineas!" shouted Jake. "Last offer, or we takes 'em back!"
Suddenly, a deep, determined voice from the quayside rang out.
"*Fifty* guineas for the pair!"

Jessica and Jamie slowly turned...
...and gazed down the gang-plank...
...and who they saw standing there made them look
at one another in absolute amazement!

Surely it *couldn't* be!
Could it?

Chapter 20

It was him! It had to be! The shimmering, long black cloak, the long black boots with the silver buckles and the pointed toes, the cane with the silver top, the scarlet waistcoat! The chalky face with the bloodshot eyes! It just *had* to be the tourist guide they'd met on the Abbey Steps! The tall, angular man dressed as *Count Dracula...*
but this time without the fangs and the bat...and wearing a tall, grey top-hat which hid his swept back, shiny, jet black hair.
And, once again, just as had happened on the Abbey Steps, both children instantly knew that there was *something* about him that they recognised from even *before* they'd set out on their journey to Whitby! They both knew him from *somewhere else*, but they couldn't quite think *where*!
"And who, may I ask, are you?" barked Captain Scraggs.
The gentleman smiled.
"Bertram Crackitt, sir! Owner and Ring-Master of the one-and-only, World famous, spectacular '*Crackitt's Circus and Freak Show*'!
And these two young specimens will go down a treat! A real treat! Especially dressed in *that* attire!"
With a flourish, he swept off his top-hat, revealing his *Count Dracula* hair, and deeply bowed.
"Bertram Crackitt, at your service!" he repeated. "So how much did we

agree? Was it *fifty* guineas for the pair?"
"We agreed on now't!" barked Scraggs. "But make it *sixty* and you can 'ave 'em!"
"They're not yours to sell, Scraggs!" suddenly snapped Jake. "They're our catch! We're doin' the sellin'!"
Then he looked at Mr Crackitt with a glint in his eye.
"We'll settle on sixty, but the money goes to *us*...not *him*! Got it?"
The circus owner agreed and as he delved into his pocket and counted out the money, the captain stormed off towards the *Neptune's* quarter-deck.
"Mark m'words!" he barked. "Them nippers'll be now't but trouble! And as for yon ruffians, we set sail on the tide! Get yourselves about yer jobs!"

Jessica and Jamie could hardly believe what was going on! They felt like they were in a cattle-market being bargained and haggled over like a pair of prize bulls! One moment they were about to become sea-dogs living on maggotty biscuits...the next, exhibits in a circus freak show! Could all this be really happening?
They stood on the quayside next to their new master, wondering whether or not to make a run for it!
"So the circus business is doing well?" asked Jake as he stuffed Crackitt's paper money into his pocket.
"With Hudson's new steam railway coming to Whitby next year, there'll be a flood of travellers! Thousands more than come by four-in-hand! And what, with Old King Bill about to pop his clogs, and young Princess Vic taking the throne...we're in for lots of celebrations! That's where m' circus comes in! Folk'll want entertainin'! Even by these two!"

And, with that, the peculiar trio made its way back along the quayside towards the draw-bridge. Near one of the stage-coach inns, Mr Crackitt motioned to the children to sit down on a heap of lobster-pots.
Jessica and Jamie wondered what was coming next!
Would Crackitt sell them in the market place to the highest bidder? Would they land up working in a factory, down a coal-mine or being stuffed up sooty chimneys. Perhaps Mr Hudson, or whatever he was

called, could use them in one of his railway building navvy gangs!
Or perhaps a highway-man would suddenly appear and kidnap them!
Or perhaps a kind, wealthy old lady might take pity on them and whisk them off to London in a stage-coach!
The children hadn't a clue what was going to happen ...but when it finally *did*...they nearly collapsed with the shock!

Mr Crackitt stood in front of them and smiled.

Jessica and Jamie gazed into the bloodshot eyes set in his pale, chalky face. They looked like rubies tossed on to freshly fallen snow.
Instantly they both thought of Chandar!
Her ruby eyes and her snow white fur!
Chandar!
Cold and dead on the Moors.
Mr Crackitt shook his head from side to side.
"Chandar is *not* dead! She still lives in the Forest!" he said in his deep, warm voice.
Jessica and Jamie were astonished!
They couldn't believe what they'd just heard!
How did this man in Whitby in the *Nineteenth Century* know about Chandar and where she lived? How did he know what they were thinking when they looked into his blood-flushed eyes?
"But she can't be! We saw her die!" Jessica exclaimed.
"A lorry hit her!" burst Jamie. "We moved her dead body away from the road!"
Crackitt paused and took a breath.
He had a difficult story to tell.
"I was Chandar!" he began. "Just a moment before the lorry hit her, my magic released me from that disguise. But I followed you to Whitby in the form of an owl. Then I became the tourist guide, *Count Dracula*, as you explored the Abbey Steps! Did you enjoy your ice-creams, by the way? And now, in the year *1835*, I am a circus owner, Mr Bertram Crackitt!"
The children's mouths fell wider and wider open.
"But...but!" they chorused.
Mr Crackitt looked at them both and rested his hands on their shoulders.
"I have been with you all the time!" he said quietly. "Queen Venetia

summoned me to be your guardian on your Quest to find your father and *Deer Leap*! The magic has been with you all the way! You don't think the Queen would have allowed you to embark on such a dangerous venture without some kind of protection? Do you?"
Jessica and Jamie were speechless.
They just stared into the Magician's eyes, completely and utterly astonished!
And it was at that very moment that they both realised where they'd seen him before!
Of course, it was Lucius!
The Magician who'd taken on Merlyn and turned him into an Eagle Owl!
The Magician who had been *Spook*, the white cat with the twitching tail!
The Magician who had taken on the *Shym-ryn* at Stonehenge.
The Magician who they thought was quietly back in *Aqua Crysta*, married to Grizelda!
"But...but! How...?" stuttered Jessica, totally confused.
Lucius grabbed a lobster-pot and sat down on it in front of them.
He looked at them intently.
"There will be plenty of time to answer your questions later, but for now, listen carefully! Your first deed is to get back to your father at Saltwick Bay. The tide will be at its fullest in less than an hour. If you make haste you can get back over the rocks before they are awash. The *Shym-ryn's* magic has him in their grasp and they are in league with the devilish and powerful *Grykes*. For a reason we do not know, their leader, *The Golphin*, wants to bargain with Queen Venetia for your father's safe return. You two have been drawn into their magic to increase his bargaining power. What lies ahead is unknown and perilous, but take comfort in knowing that the magic of *Aqua Crysta* will be victorious in the end! We will soon have your father, *Deer Leap* and you two...back where you all belong!"
"Will you be with us?" asked Jessica, at last finding her voice.
Lucius nodded his head slowly.
"The magic of the *Shym-ryn* and the *Grykes* together is very potent and powerful. But I will be with you! Of that be assured! But for now, let us make haste. I will see you to the rocks!"

By the time they reached the last red-tiled and thatched cottages of Whitby, the tide had already covered many of the seaweed covered rocks. Jessica and Jamie said farewell to Lucius and glanced for one last time over the Old Whitby of the year *1835*.
It was an incredible sight, still full of grimy, fishy, oily, smoky hustle and bustle amid the horses and carts and the manic maze of rigging rope and white sails!
Then, with a last wave to the Magician, they set off, scrambling over the slippery rocks towards Saltwick, with just one thought filling their minds!
Their father!
They could hardly wait to set eyes on him and feel his strong arms hugging them!
They just hoped he was well!

Lucius waved as he turned and wandered back into the noisy mayhem.
The Sun was sinking in the sky.
Soon it would be dark.
His mission to watch over the children from now on would be even more difficult. At the bottom of the Abbey Steps he turned left into a narrow alley.
He crept into a secluded doorway, leaned his silver-topped cane on the brickwork by the little wooden door and wrapped himself in his long, black cloak.
Then he whispered words of enchantment to himself.
In a moment he'd vanished!
Gone, lost in the magic!
Only the cane remained, leaning on the wall by the door.
The door opened and a grubby, urchin of a child, a dirty faced boy with an untidy bush of grimy, fair hair, stepped cautiously out from a small, gloomy, candle-lit room. He noticed Crackitt's cane.

"Ma, one of them posh folk's left a stick! It's got a silver top!"
"Fetch it in, son! It could be worth a shillin' or two! And be quick and shut t'door! Yon wind's gettin' chilly!"

The same chill wind was blowing over the sands as Jessica and Jamie reached Saltwick Bay. The going suddenly became easier as they ran across the beach, heading past the mouth of the cavern and towards the little lonely cottage.
Excitement pounded in their chests, as the ramshackle, tumbledown hovel came closer and closer.
They couldn't wait!

At long, long last, they were going to see their father again!

Chapter 21

"Dad! Dad!" shouted Jamie against the strengthening wind.
There was no answer.

"Dad, where are you?" called Jessica, the sky by now almost black.
But there was still no answer.
He *had* to be there somewhere!
The Saltwicks had said he was chained to the place!
Perhaps he was asleep inside.
With hearts beating faster and faster, the children crept around to the front of the weather-beaten cottage.
In the darkness they could just make out a wooden veranda, half buried by sand, shingle and shells, a battered old rowing boat and dozens and dozens of ammonites scattered everywhere.
They peeped through a paneless window...
...and there, in the dusky twilight, they saw it!
And their hearts fell like stones!!

A thick chain lay wound across the sandy floor...one end wrapped and padlocked around one of the wooden posts that held

the roof up...the other end with an iron foot manacle, stretched wide open, with a matching key tossed into the sand.
Their father had been moved from the cottage...or had he escaped? There was no telling.
The children, crest-fallen and dejected, their excitement extinguished in a flash, pushed open the cottage door and entered what had been their father's prison cell for months.
There was just the simplest of wooden furniture...a square table with a tree stump as a chair. Embers of a fire slightly glowed under a hole in the roof and rough sheets of cloth strewn on the floor formed a bed under the window. There was an axe and piles of firewood, a cooking pot, a bucket, a knife and a wooden platter. And that was it!

"Come on! We've got to go after him?" shouted Jamie.
"But where do we go? The trail's run cold!" replied Jessica. "He could have been taken out to sea, into Whitby, further south along the coast towards Robin Hood's Bay! Who knows? The ammonite clues have stopped stone dead!"

But then, as though the magic had ears and was listening to every word, Jamie pointed to the sandy floor of the cottage. There were ammonites scattered everywhere, but near the embers, was a trio of larger ones. As the children looked at them, they began to glow, silvery at first and then brilliant white. Jessica and Jamie shielded their eyes as the brilliance blazed even brighter! So bright that everything in the little room seemed to melt into one bedazzling, pure white glare. It was like being in a white hot furnace but without the heat!
Then the children heard crackling and they could smell burning.
With their hands over their eyes, they squinted through the bars of their fingers...and before them they could see rough, jagged grooves being carved into the spirals of the ancient fossils by some kind of magical beams! Three of them, one for each ammonite!
One after the other, they sizzled and etched into the spirals until they had done their work.

Then they stopped, the crackling and spitting ceased, the brilliant white faded, and the little room returned to its usual dark drabness.
And there, for the children to see clearly, was a message!
Three words they had seen before.
At the top of the well.
"*The...Golphin...Awaits*!"

The journey back across the crescent shaped remains of the tide flooded beach was easy despite the darkness, but as the children entered the Saltwicks' cavern, they began to wonder what lay ahead. Would the knee-high Saltwicks be friendly or hostile? After all, they had just lost their leader. Would they blame that on the arrival of the giants from the Upper World, Jessica and Jamie?
And what about venturing up the steps and through the door that Lady Celestine had told them about? What would they encounter on the other side? Is that where their father was? They weren't sure, but they hoped for another trio of ammonites to re-assure them. And even if they were on the right trail, how were they going to cope with the thousands of tiny, ferocious, armed Goblins? And what was *The Golphin* himself going to be like?
They both shuddered at the thought!

Cautiously, they turned into the mouth of the cavern and left the wind and the waves behind. Before them was the huddle of cottages bordering the stream. Candlelight flickered in the windows and smoke drifted lazily up from the chimneys.
All seemed quiet and peaceful.
There were no signs of the Saltwick folk at all!
Luck was on their side.
They tip-toed onwards past the giant anchor and past piles of ammonites and cockles and mussels. Past tangles of netting.
The steps were just ahead.
They crept on, keeping their fingers crossed that they wouldn't be spotted.
Quietly they stole further and further into the cavern.
So far so good!
On and on.

One foot soundlessly after the other.
Just a little further and they'd be there!
Up the steps to the door...and away from *one* danger...
...and probably straight into the grip of *another*!!
Jessica reached the staircase first.
She put one foot gingerly on the bottom step...
...and then, suddenly, as though she'd set off an invisible alarm...
...a fearsome noise thundered through the cavern!
Dogs!
Six or seven of them at least!
Savage barking and growling from some distance away in the village!
Then they heard angry voices ring out, echoing over the roof tops.
"*There they are*! *After them*!"
"*Don't let them escape*!"
"*They'll pay for the death of Celestine*!"
Jamie looked in horror towards the bridge over the stream.
He could see half-a-dozen enormous dogs, wolf-size and wolf-looking, tearing over the bridge...each dog with a rider...a helmeted, armed Saltwick! The cavalry was after them!
"Sis, I don't think talking's going to work *this* time!" he yelled.
"Come on, leg it as sharpish as you can!"
Up the steps they pelted as fast as their feet could carry them.
The dogs were already catching up!
They'd reached the steps!
Slavering and yelping from the excitement of the hunt, the dogs sensed the scent of the children and raced up the stony staircase, urged on by their manic riders whipping them on and kicking their flanks with flying boot heels!
On and on, the steps climbed out of the cavern.
Jessica and Jamie were becoming weaker and weaker by the second.
They tried to take two or even three steps at a time.
Sweat poured down their faces!
Their legs were turning to jelly!!
They were panting and gasping with every laboured lunge up the never-ending stairway!

Where was the cursed door?
And now, just below them, the scent of sweat in their nostrils, the pack of wolf-dogs was closing in for the kill!
Closer and closer!
Closer and closer!
Wild snarling and howling filled the children's ears!
Together with the clink of armour, whip cracks and frenzied screams of revenge!
Suddenly, Jessica tripped, stumbled and fell across the rough steps.
Jamie ploughed into her and tumbled over her sprawling body.
On hands and knees they scrambled panic-stricken from one step to the next!
They glanced behind them at the slavering jaws and gnashing, blood-thirsty teeth that were almost upon them!
The wild, bearded riders shouted their final threats!
The dogs were upon their prey!
The children would be torn apart in seconds!

The *Quest* was over!

Chapter 22

As the first sharp, steely canines sank deep and tore savagely into the rubber soles of their trainers, Jessica grabbed Jamie's hand and screamed with terror at their attackers, tears flooding down her face, mingling with her sweat. She summoned all the strength she could muster and swung her other fist at the dogs and then tried her best to roll over onto her young brother to protect him. Jamie kicked and kicked at the snapping jaws, but it was all of no use. The lead dog, urged onwards by its wild, hysterical rider, snarled and bit at his flaying ankles, until, at last, it caught one between its razor teeth. Jamie yelled out with pain and Jessica lashed out with her clenched fists. She landed a blow on the dog's cheek, as another clenched its teeth around her elbow!

As her screams of anguished pain joined her brother's...they both knew it was all over. Death would be with them in mo...

And then, they heard it!

The march of hundreds of feet...coming down the stairs above them!

The rhythmic, dull thud, thud, thud of the gleaming, metallic boots of the *Grykes*!

The Goblin army was pouring down the steps, again like a volcanic flow of silver lava...drawn swords, pointed spears and taut stringed bows at the ready!

"*Back, back, down the steps*!" called the Saltwick leader of the pack.

"*Retreat*! *Retreat*!" echoed his second-in-command.
The dogs whimpered and cut short their savagery.
Their brutal assault was ended, their bloody meal denied.
Tails between legs, the half-wild beasts bounded down the staircase and back to the village.
The six riders knew they were no match for the Goblins.
The *Grykes* had re-captured their prey.
Talk about '*out of the frying-pan and into the fire*'!

Like on the beach, before the gang of sailors had rescued them, Jessica and Jamie were surrounded. The torrent of *Grykes* swept around them smoothly and cut off any escape down the steps, not that they had any intentions of following the dogs!
Then a narrow passage-way was made on the staircase lined by the diminutive Goblins, not one taller than a pencil. It led upwards.

The children staggered to their feet, their wounds throbbing, and stumbled up the steps. In the distance they could see the magnificent door.
It was enormous, like a gateway into a castle...arched and in two great halves, made from panels of dark wood dotted with iron studs. In front was a portcullis, a heavy, gridded iron lattice-work, protecting the door itself.
As the children limped up the steps, the portcullis was raised with an eerie grating sound. Then both halves of the great door opened with a series of creaking groans.
Jessica and Jamie looked at one another as they passed under the portcullis and through the doorway.
They had entered the '*Land of the Grykes*'!
They wondered whether or not they would ever see the light of day again...let alone their father!

The Underworld beyond the door was surprisingly beautiful! Surprising because the children expected a cold, grim, harsh Land in keeping with the cold, grim, harsh *Grykes*! But instead, they found a strange resemblance to *Aqua Crysta*! It seemed warm and friendly, perhaps because it was nothing like the rough, stony, dripping caverns where the Saltwicks lived. Here the walls were of milky pink crystals with forests of glowing pink and red stalactites hanging from the roofs of the caves and passages. The light the rock produced was very much the same as *Aqua Crystan* light.

It appeared that the children were walking through a long, main cave with smaller caves leading off on both sides. It was wide enough for the Goblins to usher them forwards by a never-ending, metallic flow behind and to the sides of the children...shepherding them onwards like hundreds of sheep-dogs!

The floor sloped gently, and the roof of the main cave was high enough for the children to walk upright without stooping. The longest of the stalactites was well beyond their reach. It strangely felt like walking through *Aqua Crysta* as a full-sized person!

After a while they began to notice doorways and windows cut into the crystal rock, leading into excavated rooms...but far too large to be houses for the *Grykes*. They seemed to be mostly abandoned, although several had been sub-divided inside by two or three wooden floors. And each storey was divided further into several smaller rooms, presumably to accommodate the Goblins!

Jessica and Jamie began to think that the *Grykes* had shrunk over the generations, rather like the Saltwicks. Probably something to do with the *Crystals of Eternity* that had plunged to Earth from the far depths of the Universe thousands of years ago!

On and on they trudged until they reached a peculiar shaped, crystal water-pump in the middle of the cave passage.

The children's eyes suddenly lit up with hope!

The handle and the spout were made of wood, but embedded in the

pinky-rose crystals were three dark ammonites! It was clear that they were *still* on the trail!

Just beyond the pump, they came to a large square hole in the floor like a trap-door without the door! A column of *Grykes* swarmed fluidly past to stop them from going any further. Jessica and Jamie took the hint from the wordless troops that they had to descend the ladder which they could see protruding from the gaping hole.

Jessica led the way and stepped down the half-a-dozen wooden rungs

into the cool, swirling water of a shallow stream, lit pink by the luminous rocks of another passage-way. Three more ammonites in the wall indicated the way, and on the children swished through the water, still wearing their trainers and not even bothering to roll up their jeans. The water almost seemed to soothe and heal their wounds.

Suddenly they realised that the horde of Goblin guards had left them...deserted them! They'd stayed behind at the top of the ladder, presumably their job done!

Once again the children felt strangely alone in an alien World. Without the marching boots of the soldiers it became spookily

quiet, although the children didn't exactly miss their captors!

On and on they splashed until they reached the end of the tunnel and found themselves at the top of a waterfall. Opposite were two more waterfalls, separated by a cliff face with yet another trio of ammonites. Below them was a cave entrance with a staircase. A narrow path took them down behind one of the cascades to the cave entrance. They climbed the stairs and came to the 'bridge-keeper's' cottage beneath the largest ammonite the children had ever seen! It was easily four times the height of the cottage, and had another couple of smaller ones for company! They peeped into the cottage but it was deserted like everywhere else! There wasn't a single soul to be seen.

The children walked over a swaying, hammocky rope bridge which crossed a deep cavern half-way between a mass of stalactites above and a wide floor beneath. From the bridge they could just make out a half-buried, horned helmet on the floor of the cavern, and by following several staircases they soon reached it.

As they looked at the helmet with its jewel encrusted rim and fierce Viking horns, they realised that the houses surrounding them in the cavern were much smaller than the earlier ones...more in keeping with the size of the Goblins. The helmet would have easily fitted Jamie's head twice over and a dozen *Grykes* could have sat between its horns! Perhaps it was an ancient relic...a sort of monument reminding the Goblins of the size they used to be in the past.

The children followed the level, wide floor of the deserted cavern until they came to another flight of steps. And it was at this point that they just stopped...and stood...and stared! Before them was an amazing scene! To go with the helmet, a long, elegant shimmering silver sword with a gem-packed handle swept down the centre of the

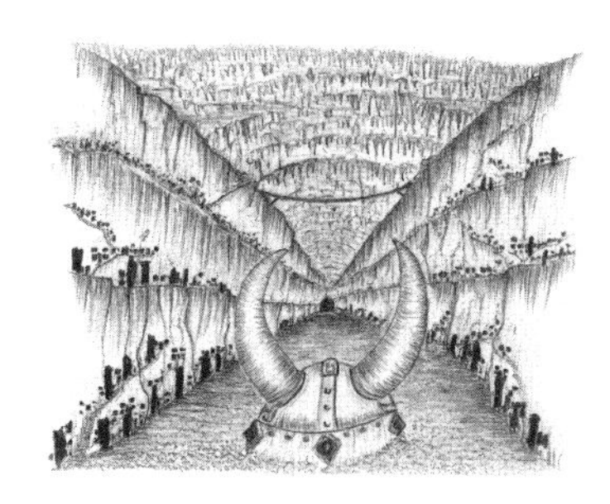

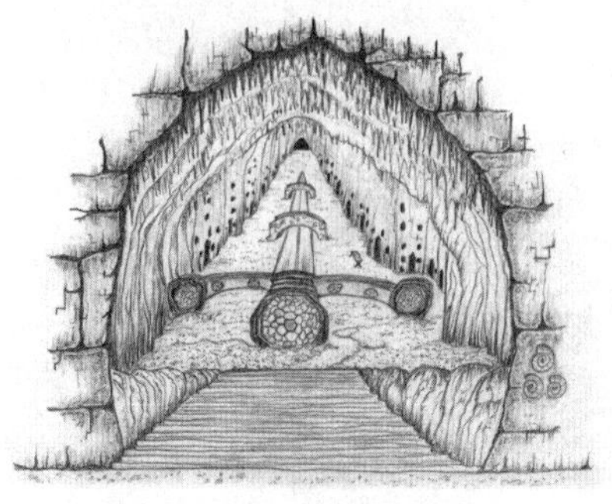

next part of the cavern...crossed and held down by two small, stone bridges.
It was a brilliant sight and held Jessica and Jamie in awe, as they sat and rested on the top step of the staircase.
They could have gazed and wondered at the view for hours, but they knew they just *had* to carry on!
Surely *soon* they would come across the Goblins again and their giant leader, *The Golphin*...and *that* is where they hoped they'd find their father and even *Deer Leap*!

They plodded on, along the length of the sword, and began to notice that the cavern was becoming larger and larger, the stalactite roof higher and higher!
Somehow the sword suddenly seemed longer than it should have been, in comparison to the helmet! Jamie couldn't possibly have picked it up!
Strange thoughts began to enter the children's minds!
Were things becoming *bigger*...?
...Or were *they* becoming *smaller*?
Were the same magical, shrinking mists here, as they were in *Aqua Crysta*?
They were questions they had neither time nor energy to ponder.

But, when they suddenly came to the cavern's dead end, the terrifyingly monstrous answer was staring them in the face!

For there they lay, towering menacingly above them!
Defiantly blocking their way!

How could they possibly go on?

Chapter 23

As Jessica and Jamie gazed at the vast, titanic, spiralling fossil that towered before them, it almost took their breaths away! Surely this was the greatest, most gigantic ammonite the World had ever seen!

They'd thought the ammonite at the bridge-keeper's cottage had been *big*!...but this one was definitely in a whole new league of its own!

And, what's more, *seven* other giants surrounded the whopper, just keeping it company.

The Magnificent Eight!

But what fascinated and puzzled the children even more was...the ladder!

A rope ladder with wooden rungs that stretched temptingly from the rough ground at the end of the cavern to the very centre of the giant ammonite.

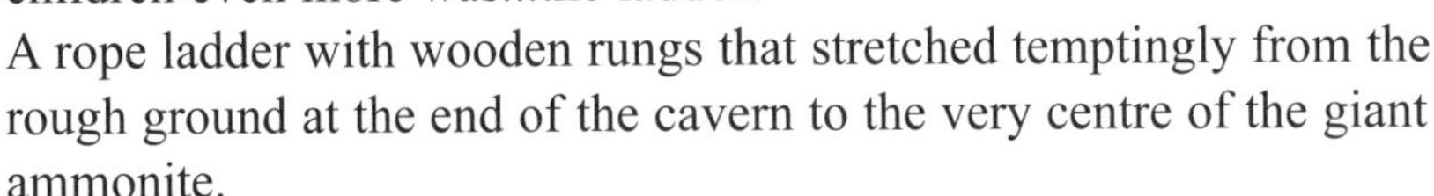

"It's no good staring at it, we've got to climb it!" burst Jamie, as his sister's eyes gazed at the awesome sight.

"Their shiny blackness and sheer size seems so evil and frightening and...and...*final*!" whispered Jessica. "It's as though we've come to the

end of *one* World...and the ladder will take us to *another*!"
"Come on, Jess! We've got to go!" urged Jamie, grabbing hold of his sister's hand.

And with that, the children began the nerve-racking, and somewhat wobbly, climb to the beckoning, central eye of the gargantuan fossil. The ladder was tilted at an angle, somewhere half-way between horizontal and vertical...like a bridge with a slope. Crawling up it on all fours was tricky and there was always the thought that the whole thing might just flip over at any moment! The children took their time, all the while getting closer and closer to the shiny, spiralling cliff that seemed to almost spin before their eyes, making them dizzy and even more wobbly! Slowly but surely they inched along, gripping the swaying ropes tighter and tighter. Soon they were half-way across and they paused for a rest. Then they carried on, higher and higher off the ground and closer and closer to the beguiling black eye. As the last, gleaming, jet-black spiral seemed to wrap itself around them and suck them in, it almost felt as if the giant ammonite was alive and was swallowing them whole!
At long last they reached the end of the ladder and stepped off onto a narrow platform. Before them was a round, black emptiness, devoid of all traces of light. The children each took a deep breath and, with Jessica in the lead, they began to walk gingerly forwards, their arms outstretched, feeling the way, like butterfly antennae.
But there was nothing to feel!
It was just a black emptiness!
They could have stepped over the edge of a precipice at any moment!
Anxiously, they began to shuffle and inch into the dark, their eyes wide open but seeing absolutely nothing!
And it was so quiet, so very quiet!
All they could hear were their own heartbeats and the scraping of their rubber soles on the gritty rock.
On and on...and then...
Jessica suddenly stopped.
She could smell the sea.
And the floor felt slippery!

Then, in the pitch black, she screamed a short, blood-curdling scream!
Something had touched her face.
Something soggy and slimy...and smelly!
"Sea-weed!" she suddenly shouted. "Hanging from above us in the dark!"
Soon they were both enclosed in a thick curtain of the smothering stuff, breathlessly battling their way through. It seemed never-ending...and then...through squinted eyes, they could make out the first, welcome glimmers of light...pale greeny-blue, turquoise light...filtering its way through the dense, sea-weed barrier.
More and more of the enticing rays of light met the children and beckoned them onwards, as they fought their way through the wet, salty, clinging weed...until, at last, they thankfully let the final strands slither over their shoulders...and emerged from the curtain...
And there, rolling out from beneath their feet into the far distance was a scene that set their pulses racing and their eyes manically dancing and darting everywhere!
It was like nothing on Earth!
A huge, marine World of every possible shade of blue...all before them under a gigantic, sloping roof of translucent crystal, like a sheet of thick, solid ice. The light was coming from above...passing through the crystal and illuminating all that lay beneath. And above the crystal roof, the children could see blurred, moving shapes...shoals of fish, single fish, jelly fish...swimming in the sea...actually *above* their heads! They had emerged into an Undersea World! They were standing on dry land *beneath* the sea...with a sea-bed made from solid crystal, dotted with rocks crowned with swaying, floating sea-weed streaming in the currents like flowing hair in the breeze.
Fish were swimming between them...and seals...and gannets and puffins soaring through the salt-water after prey!
And it was all happening above their heads!
And through the sea water, above who knows what depths...or heights...was the sky...and the clouds...and the Sun!
Great, wide, dazzling patches of shimmering water sparkled and danced, silhouetting the sea-creatures swimming below!
It was a stunning scene!

"It must be *so* thick! To hold up the sea!" said Jamie dreamily, his eyes straining through the glassy crystal, watching lobsters scrabbling across the sea-bed chasing crabs.

"It's absolutely fantastic!" whispered Jessica, lost in the sea-scape above her head, looking at sea-urchins and anemones from below! "We're actually *under* the sea, and *under* the sea-bed!"

And as if *that* wasn't enough...the Land that stretched out before them in the shape of a gigantic, sloping, open fan, was equally, if not *more* magical! It was a World of countless, flat, smooth, silvered islands separated by an ocean of tropical-looking turquoise. The water was perfectly still.

There were no waves...just ripples...coming from the drips from the crystal ceiling. Every time a drip dropped and plunged into the tranquil turquoise, circles within circles sprung across the water merging from ripples hatched from other plunging drips.

Around the edge of the fan, clinging to rock faces were hundreds of strange flowers, the like of which the children had never seen in their lives! Their colours and shapes were so elegant and exotic. Some even seemed to be breathing bubbles of gas into the humid, submarine atmosphere! Then from behind one particularly luxuriant blush of purply-pink flowers they saw a fabulous creature emerge which made them gasp with surprise!

It was a sea-horse! Greeny-blue and about the size of a *Gryke*, but instead of hovering in water, it was hovering in the air by fluttering little wings...and breathing out great clouds of bubbles like the flowers!

More and more appeared, all seeming to enjoy hovering around the flowers like giant humming birds!
"Some have reins around their necks!" whispered Jessica.
"Perhaps the Goblins ride them, like we ride the crystalids back home!"

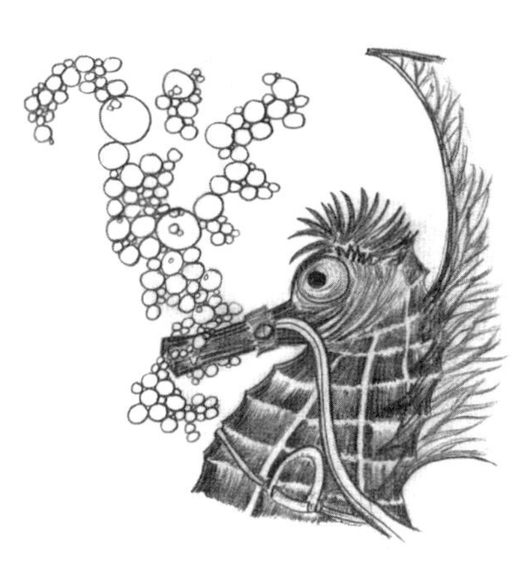

In the far distance, the crystal roof dipped and seemed to meet the smooth sea-water. It was as if the Undersea World was shaped like a giant, transparent, hollow wedge of Wensleydale cheese! The children were standing in a little hole in its thick edge, looking towards its tapering end!
"It's so quiet again!" whispered Jessica. "There's no sign of *anybody* living here!"
But she couldn't have been more wrong!
For just then, the children spotted a glint of movement coming from one of the flat islands!
They strained their eyes to look at one of the discs of silver.
Then they noticed it again!
A strange, swaying movement, with sunlight from the sea and sky glinting on the metallic surface.
It was as though the island was alive and its silvered skin was creeping!
And then a cold, shiver ran up their spines!
And the hairs, once more, stood up on the back of their necks!
The island *was* alive!!
It was covered with *Grykes*!
Every possible square inch was cloaked and plated in metal, without a single gap!
And *every* island was the same!
They were *all* absolutely flooded with the Goblins, standing silently, shoulder-to-shoulder and absolutely statue-still!

All that is, except for *one* particular island!
An island in the far distance, where the crystal roof was lower, and a narrow waterfall gurgled just beyond, seemingly linking the sea above with the Underworld.
This island was different!

For rising from it...was a huge rocky throne.
And upon it sat *one* enormous Goblin!
It was staring straight back at the children, icily meeting their gaze.

'*The Golphin*', at last!!

Chapter 24

From their balcony looking out over the Undersea *Kingdom of the Grykes*, the children watched and waited, wondering what was going to happen next. *The Golphin*, it seemed had noticed *them*...but all remained quiet and peaceful, with just the sound of dripping water echoing around the blue. The only movements were the ripples, radiating smoothly, the swaying flowers and the gently hovering sea-horses.

Across the still, metallic islands, the *King of the Goblins* seemed just the same as his thousands of subjects...just maybe three or four times larger! It was hard to tell because of the distance, but the children could make out his pointed features, his armour and his enormous golden helmet with ram's horns on each side...looking like golden ammonites!

Suddenly and completely unexpectedly, a deep voice rang out, shattering the silence.

"Greetings!" the word rumbled around the tranquil, turquoise World beneath the sea. "I have been waiting for you for some time!"

Jessica and Jamie stared into the distance.

The Golphin stood up from his throne and walked slowly over to what appeared to be a large, angular box shape, several times his height and equally wide. It seemed to be draped in a loosely fitting, sparkling green cloth.

The voice thundered out again.
"Is *this* what you have travelled so far to set your eyes upon?"
The giant Goblin reached for a cord and pulled.
At once, the green cloth slithered to the ground...
...and there...in a glass box...was a wall-less room!!
A room that Jessica and Jamie knew all too well!
Furnished exactly as they'd left it back in the Summer!
It was *Deer Leap's* living-room...and there, sitting in his favourite armchair, eating a bowl of cereal and gazing at a television without a picture...was *their father*!!
"Dad! Dad!" shouted Jessica across the blue.
"Dad! Can you hear us! Can you see us!" shouted Jamie.
The Golphin laughed a deep laugh.
Then his voice rattled through the Land again.
"He cannot do either! He is trapped in the magic of the *Grykes* and the *Shym-ryn* working as one! Such magic is invincible, unconquerable! There is no magic strong enough to defeat us! *Nothing* will re-unite you with your father until our demands are met!! *Nothing*!"

On the word '*Nothing*', a dark shadow crept gracefully across the turquoise World and came to rest across several islands.
The children gazed up through the crystal roof, as did thousands of *Grykes* and their King.

An ominous, giant, black shape had come to rest among the sparkle and glitter of the sea.
It was the hull of a huge ship!
An enormous anchor plummeted through the clear sea amid a swash of bubbles and crashed silently onto the crystal sea-bed, scattering lobsters and crabs.
Suddenly, a crimson beam shot through the water, through the crystal roof, and through the damp, warm air of the Undersea World. It lit a broad disc of crimson around the Goblin King and his glass box.
Then another deep voice rang out across the Kingdom.

It seemed to be coming from above.
"*The Golphin* is mistaken!" the voice from the salty heavens began.
"There *is* a magic that *will* conquer that of the *Grykes* and the *Shym-ryn* even if they work together as one! And I am here as a practitioner of it! But first tell me of your demands!"
The Golphin returned to his throne and addressed the heavens.
His voice was still commanding and unbending!
"First, let it be known, that I, *The Golphin*, will *not* be threatened by your idle boasts, whoever you are! I repeat! There is *no* magic strong enough to defeat us! Your only hope is that I can bargain with the magical Realm of *Aqua Crysta* and its Queen, the *Queen Venetia*!"
"What is your demand?" came the voice from above, rather impatiently.
The Golphin paused and looked around him, slightly sadly.
"Our World, the *Kingdom of the Grykes*, is slowly drowning under the water which leaks incessantly from the sea! You witness before you a scene of many islands burdened with my people! Once there were no islands, but the slow rising of the brine has reduced us to what you see! Soon the islands will be drowned and even the *Old Caverns* where we used to live before we lost our stature! I am in search of a place of refuge! A Land that will welcome us! Away from the leaking sea! Such a Land is the *Realm of Aqua Crysta*! It is said that its people number just a handful compared to my thousands! *Aqua Crysta* must become our place of refuge! It is safe beneath the Forest, away from the dreaded sea!
I must meet and bargain with the *Queen Venetia*! My demand is that in return for the father of Jessica and Jamie, the whole of the home they call *Deer Leap* and the children themselves...I and my people will be welcome in her *Realm*...as, indeed, many people have been, for centuries!!"
At that moment, from behind the sea-weed curtain, a familiar tide of *Gryke* soldiers swept around the feet of the children and held them with drawn swords, spears and bows.
There was a nervous silence.
Then the voice from above spoke again.
"First, I will show you the strength and power of *my* magic. That of *Aqua Crysta*!"

The Golphin looked upwards shielding his eyes from the crimson beam.
"*What* do you show me!" he called with a disbelieving smirk in his voice.
In a flash of even brighter crimson, the glass box and its contents vanished before the very eyes of the Goblin King!
The Golphin looked astonished!
And so did Jessica and Jamie!
Then the voice from the watery heavens spoke out once more.
"I am speaking from a vessel floating above your *Kingdom*! The good ship '*Neptune*' from Whitby harbour! Can you see her hull?"
Jessica and Jamie just *couldn't* believe their eyes...nor their ears!
It was Lucius! He must have jumped aboard the ship and told Captain Scraggs where to sail as the vessel left Whitby!
And that's exactly what had happened! A huddle of confused sailors led by Jake were held prisoner on the deck clumped around the main sail, held in rigid magical bonds that had been cast by Lucius...and the bewildered Captain Scraggs himself was tied to the steering wheel following the Magician's strict orders!
"I have made it known to the Queen Venetia that you wish to bargain with her!" Lucius went on. "I have also magicked her ship, the '*Goldcrest*', to bring the Queen to meet with you! She will be alone, other than a small unarmed crew. Captain Frumo will steer the ship into the harbour at Whitby at midnight on All Hallow's Eve, at a time *one hundred and seventy years* hence forward. The Queen will be at her prow. You be at the harbour bridge in the town and a bargain can be struck!"
Another silence followed.
"How can I be sure that I can trust you?" came the voice of *The Golphin* at last.
"And how can *I* be sure that *I* can trust *you*?" replied Lucius from the heavens. "But meanwhile, I will take away *another* of your bargaining pieces! Jessica and Jamie! Brace yourselves!!"
Another beam of crimson shot through the sea and the crystal roof. This time aimed at the children perched on the edge of their rocky balcony.
The Goblin King stared in astonishment, as his brand new captives vanished!

In an instant!
Gone into the magic!
And they didn't feel a thing!

But the very next moment, to their complete and utter shock, the children looked around in total bewilderment!
They were in the cellar beneath the Abbey Steps!!
Surrounded by the very same barrels they had explored, what seemed like centuries ago!
The same street light stood by the entrance with its warm, orange glow.
All was quiet...except for a scraping and a shuffling behind one of the heaps of wooden barrels.
Jamie looked at his sister and put a finger to his lips!
"Ssshh!" he whispered. "I'll creep over and investigate!"
"Be careful!" whispered Jessica. "It could be the *Gryke* troops who live up here!"
But before he could move an inch, they heard it!
Another sound!
Coming from the Victorian street beyond the lamp-post!
The rhythmic, dull beat of hundreds of metal boots!

The Goblin army was on the march yet again!

Chapter 25

Jessica and Jamie hid behind a heap of barrels and watched as the small number of cellar troops emerged from the cracks in the walls. Quickly the Goblins worked the mechanism which opened the stone door that led out onto the cobbles of Donkey Road. Slowly it grated open and moonlight streamed in.

Then the Goblins darted back into the shadows and waited for their countrymen. Meanwhile, the incessant thud, thud of the massed soldiers from below was becoming louder and louder!

Louder and louder!

"It sounds as though *The Golphin's* coming up here with his whole army!" whispered Jamie.

"...To attack the *Goldcrest* and Queen Venetia!" added Jessica. "Then the whole lot of them could take the ship...and somehow, by *their* magic...get to *Aqua Crysta*!"

"How can we stop them?" asked Jamie.

"Quick, shift some barrels! Let's block the way!"

But it was too late!

Already the march of boots was in the Victorian street!

"Come on, let's make a run for it!" yelled Jessica. "Perhaps we can get down to the harbour first and warn the Queen!"
They scrambled through the gaping hole and fell into the chilly night they had left behind and back into present-day Whitby.
They got to their feet, ran down the steep Donkey Road, into Church Street and then down a side alley to the little Tate Hill pier overlooking the harbour.

Suddenly a great explosion came from the top of the Abbey Steps and the black night sky turned into day! Streaks of fireworks screamed across the darkness, and burst into huge, round blossoms of sparkling, crackling yellows and whites! Then another explosion rocked the sky! This time a giant, fiery, green and pink chrysanthemum swelled and filled the dark!
The firework show was well underway, and crowds of cheering tourists and Goths were ambling down historic Church Street, lining the harbour quays, and filling the swing-bridge. More crowds were gathered on the grass in front of the Royal Hotel high up on West Cliff! There they would have the best views.
It seemed that Whitby was heaving with people, all enjoying the Hallowe'en entertainment!
If only they'd known *what* was about to hit them!

As more great fountains of brilliant white sparks exploded and gushed into the darkness above the Abbey, lighting up the whole of the harbour, to the cheers of the crowds, the *Grykes* were already pouring into the cellar beneath the famous Steps. Every tenth soldier had been given a flaming torch from the fiery rooms under the Victorian street...and now the others grabbed even more weapons from the barrels in the cellar. Armed to the teeth, the advance troops flowed out

through the doorway beneath the red lantern lamp-post and onto Donkey Road.
With the tiny, fiery torches illuminating the way, the gleaming, silver lava streamed over the cobbles. Soon the column of soldiers had spread to the full width of the road as it flooded past the bottom of the Abbey Steps, past *Spindle-Top* cottage and into Church Street.
Meanwhile, more and more troops surged through the doorway, accompanied now by the Goblin *cavalry*!
Grykes on sea-horses! Scores of them!
Pouring in torrents through the doorway, all breathing out streams of bubbles into the chilly air. They hovered and darted forwards over the heads of the ground forces like tiny helicopters...with one giant sea-horse carrying the King Goblin himself!
"Onwards to the bridge!" he called, urging on his warriors. "Onwards to the bridge. The *Goldcrest* and *Aqua Crysta* will be mine!!"

It was then that the unstoppable river of the Goblin army met the first innocent by-standers! The unknowing families and couples of ambling holiday-makers, all happily clutching their fish and chips, candyfloss and pints of beer and staring up now and again into the night sky, as fireworks exploded overhead.
The first ones to notice anything peculiar was a young Goth couple from Huddersfield. Dressed in black veils, velvets and laces and grasping a pint of lager each, they both glanced at the advancing tide of silver, gurgling and gushing towards them down Church Street. Then they looked at one another...then into their glasses, thinking it was the drink playing tricks with their eyes! They looked back along the narrow, old street, with slightly confused expressions on their faces...somewhere between wonder and horror!!

Hundreds of pencil-high silver dwarfs!
All waving swords and spears, and bows and arrows!
Some riding sea-horses!

It was all too much!
Quietly, they calmly put their glasses on the pavement...and *ran*!!
"*Run for it*! *Run for it*!" they shrieked as they pelted into the crowds, madly waving their arms and pointing at the terror that was descending on them all, like a tidal wave!
And it was then that the real panic began!
Screaming, running, tripping, crashing and barging into one another, the tourists galloped through the market-place and towards the swing-bridge. They just had to get away from Old Whitby!
Children were picked up into parents' arms, fish and chips thrown into the air, spooky masks ripped off horror-struck faces!
But the silver army was too fast for them!
It was already swilling and bubbling around the feet of the petrified onlookers. People were pressed into doorways, up narrow alleys and even into the sea!
Doors were even broken down and crowds poured into closed shops and cafes! Anything to get out of the way of the silver tide!
It was sheer and utter pandemonium!
And throughout the mayhem, the fireworks continued to explode in the sky, and the crowds on the West-side of the river carried on cheering and clapping as though nothing out of the ordinary was happening at all!
The East-side crowd surged onto the swing-bridge, the Goblins snapping at their heels. People squealed with pain as over-enthusiastic soldiers fired hundreds of sharp, little arrows into the fleshy legs and bottoms of the public! But there was nothing anyone could do!
The tidal wave that was upon them was just too big and too forceful!!
There was no way of stopping it!
The crowds just *had* to keep moving forward.
Soon the swing-bridge was full to the brim of terrified folk...but still, the silver army kept advancing...pushing the holiday-makers over to West-side. Moments later, they'd taken and occupied the bridge completely!

Then, with brilliant timing, the bells of St Mary's struck midnight.
The fireworks stopped.
The crowds quietened and just stared open-mouthed at the swing-bridge.

It was completely awash with silver!
Completely covered in *Grykes*!
The roadway, the steel fences, the handrails the four lamp-posts, the bridge-keeper's hut!
Everything!
Even the crowds on the grassy West Cliff suddenly noticed the bridge, shining silver in the moonlight, and started pointing excitedly.
"That's brill!" said a white-faced, young Goth. "It's a good show they've put on!"
"Better than the blinkin' fireworks!" said another.
"Once you've seen one firework show, you've seen 'em all!" said another. "But a silver bridge like that takes the biscuit! Council's done brill! They ought to try it in London!"
Then something completely different caught the eyes of everyone. Heads and eyes swivelled seawards.

In the distance a ship...a vessel like a Viking longship...was heading serenely between the light-house quays, her square, yellow sail billowing in the breeze, her golden prow cutting through the calm water.

On and on, she glided into the harbour, and then banks of oars appeared on her flanks and began to slow her down. Her sail was hauled up to the cross mast and she came to a swaying halt just in front of the silvered swing-bridge.

No one on board had noticed two children on Tate Hill pier, madly waving and shouting. If they *had*, then what happened next may have been averted, and the course of history changed!
Everything would have been different!

But instead, the *Magical Realm of Aqua Crysta* was about to face its greatest tragedy...and Jessica's life would change *forever*!

Chapter 26

The crowd of happy holiday-makers perched and shivering on lofty, distant West Cliff watched keenly, stamping their feet and swinging their arms, all trying to keep warm. They thought this a wonderful conclusion to the Hallowe'en entertainment! An illuminated bridge, dressed in moon-lit, gleaming silver, with dozens of flickering flames and weird hovering, plastic sea-horses! And, not only that, but a splendid Viking ship sailing serenely into the harbour, too!
Brilliant! The organisers had done well!
A great way to follow the fireworks!
Perhaps a mystery guest was aboard the ship!
A pop-star or a film-star!
No, more likely just the Mayor of Whitby or some other dignatory!
They rubbed their cheeks and wrapped up their children...and waited... and watched!
But, on the other hand, the anxious, shaken crowds on the quayside by the swing-bridge had a totally different view!
They knew that the bridge was alive with a terrifying force that had driven them to panic and pandemonium! Tiny armoured Goblins, armed to the teeth and acting as one vast creature like a great swarm of ants or bees!
They shivered and hugged their children, *too*, but not just because of the cold!

For a minute or two, nothing happened, but then movement was spotted on the *Goldcrest*.
A regal figure could be seen walking along the deck towards the golden prow.
A woman in a flowing, green robe with a drift of long, fair hair blowing in the breeze.
A small golden coronet glinted in the moonlight.
Venetia, Queen of *Aqua Crysta*...but totally unknown to anyone!

The *King of the Goblins* bounded from his sea-horse and stood nobly on the hand-rail in the centre of the bridge, his armoured chest thrust proudly forward, his ram's horn helmet thrust high. He had a stern expression etched into his severe, angular face...his long, pointed nose, ears and chin catching the moonlight.
He looked down at the Queen and spoke,
"We have a bargain to strike, Your Majesty!" his voice rang out into the night.
The quayside crowds gasped.
"But, Sire, from what I have heard, my chief Magician, Lucius, has relieved you of your bargaining power! Is this true?" the Queen replied, looking up at the King.
Suddenly, the voices of two children could be heard from the deserted East-side, just beyond the bridge.
"It is! It is!" they chorused.
"*We* are safe!" exclaimed Jessica. "And so we think is our father...and *Deer Leap*...!"
"...Or at least one room of it!" burst Jamie.
The giant Goblin looked daggers at the children and clicked his fingers.
The massed army made one, sudden, uniform movement and the bridge shimmered in the moonlight, as though its silver skin had slid just an inch or two to the left.
The soldiers were ready! Poised for action!
"I, *The Golphin, Lord and Master of Undersea* will *never* be defeated by your magic! Venetia, I claim *your Realm* from this moment on!"
He clicked his fingers again.
Every single *Gryke* responded.

The bridge shimmered and its skin jolted again!
And then...it happened!
"*Watch out*!!" shrieked Jessica and Jamie desperately, as an enormous, wide arc of glinting silver spears and arrows sliced upwards through the air...and down into their target!
The Golphin clicked his fingers, and another silver wave arched and whooshed through the air.
Thousands and thousands of tiny, sharp points pierced the sides of the ship, her mast and her decks!
Queen Venetia stood defiantly at the prow.
"You will *never* take *Aqua Crysta*!" she thundered at her foe.
"*Never*!"
But then...in a single, swift, devastating movement at the speed of light, the Goblin King grabbed a silver spear from one of his soldiers and hurled it with all his strength at the Queen.
It flew through the air in a blur of silver.
She didn't stand a chance!
Its lethally sharp point plunged into the Queen's chest and she staggered forward, blood pouring from her wound.
"*Never*!...*Never*!...*Nev*...!" she exclaimed with her last breath.
Then she collapsed...and died!

The Queen was dead!

Jessica and Jamie gazed, horror-struck, from the side of the bridge. They had witnessed the death of their greatest friend, Queen Venetia and their hearts sank.
But within a split-second, their devastation and sorrow was diverted, their pain temporarily extinguished. Every solemn, mournful thought in their heads was suddenly bulldozed away by what happened next!

A crimson beam...wider than ever before...enveloped the whole of the swing-bridge and its silver Goblin skin! It was coming from directly above, where a moon-lit, chestnut horse...a mare, with a dark mane flowing and great swan's wings beating...could be seen hovering in the

starry sky, treading air with her flying hooves!
And, astride the regal animal's broad back, a man with a billowing, heather coloured robe and knee-length, black, sharp-toed boots with silver buckles glinting in the moonshine.
Lucius...riding a giant *Gabrielle*!
And, he too, was full of remorse and regret!
His magic had brought him *just* too late.
Too late to save his Queen!
Instead, his anger bubbled into swift *revenge*!
Another whispered word of magic fell from his lips and...
...a moment later, the silver swing-bridge vanished!
Completely!
Along with almost every single *Gryke*!
And their King!
The silver plague had been wiped out at a stroke, together with its murderous leader!
And, all at once, for a moment or two, East Whitby was cut off from the West-side. Nothing spanned the river. There was a void where a bridge should have been!
But not for long!
The magical beam changed from crimson to bright, emerald green...and the most wondrous bridge in the World formed before the onlookers' bewildered eyes! First, the remaining hundreds of *Grykes* and their sea-horses coiled into a solid band of silver ammonites which leaped across the river and acted as a sturdy foundation! Then, with invisible, magical hands working feverishly, the Esk was spanned by a wide, curving rainbow of crystals of every colour you could imagine! Finally, four towering, glassy, transparent ammonites blossomed at each end. These held the axles and mechanisms for the two halves of the brand new draw-bridge! And to prove it worked perfectly, as soon as it

was complete, the rainbow split and the two halves slowly raised and pointed towards the Magician and his chestnut steed!
But they'd vanished, too!
Along with the *Goldcrest* and Jessica and Jamie!!

The crowds of holiday-makers on West Cliff applauded and cheered! It had all been well worth the wait!
"What a show!" called a young father, his son on his shoulders.
"It's amazing what they can do with lasers, now-a-days!" exclaimed another.
"We'll be back next year to see if they can top *that*!" beamed another.

But the folk on the quayside had witnessed the whole drama at close hand.
They would never ever forget their experiences.
For them it had all been real!
They had *felt* the power of the Goblins!
They had *heard* every word that had been spoken.
They had *seen* the murder!
Now, the amazing night was over. It had come to an end.
And tomorrow, they would go back to 'life as normal'.

But for Jessica and Jamie it was all just beginning!
And, life was *never* going to be the same again!

Chapter 27

As you might have expected, a dark, sombre cloud of gloom and despair had descended across the Forest. A heavy melancholy sank through the branches and drifted amid the undergrowth. Silence reigned and the sorrow seeped and trickled through the rocks into the Magical Realm of *Aqua Crysta* itself.
Its people felt at once leaderless and, somehow, vulnerable.
Their Queen, whether foolishly or bravely, had sacrificed herself.
She had faced single-handedly, the vastness and power of the entire enemy at the bridge over the River Esk. The magic had arrived too late to help her and she had perished in a noble cause.
She would be sadly and deeply missed.

In the early morning sunshine, Jessica and Jamie sat quietly, in sorrowful thought, at the foot of a spruce tree near where *Deer Leap* should have been.
There were still no signs of it and they were beginning to think that, once again, the cottage and their father were lost in the magic...and the whole Quest had been in vain.
At least the children were delighted to see the real Chandar again, together with Strike and Gabrielle nibbling grass nearby...and were amazed by the tale Lucius told of how he'd magicked the *Goldcrest* and Queen Venetia to Whitby. It hadn't been the real *Goldcrest* after all! It had been the

splendid model that had won the competition back at the *Meeting Hall Cavern*. The ship made by Jude, the crystal-carver from Middle Floss.
"If only the Queen Venetia who died *hadn't* been the *real* Queen Venetia!" Jessica had said. But Lucius had sadly assured her that the Queen had insisted on herself taking part in the plan. It definitely *was* the *real* Queen who had died!
"If only I'd got there just moments earlier!" sighed Lucius, his emerald-green eyes downcast beneath his mane of raven-black hair.
His normally youthful, rosy cheeked face looked older and drawn.
Jessica took his hand.
"You have done brilliantly! Everything the Queen asked you to do!" she said quietly. "You followed us to the end...!"
"But, if only I could have vanished her just before *The Golphin's* spear flew through the air!" Lucius replied.
"By the way, what happened to that nasty piece of work and the rest of the *Grykes*?" chirped Jamie, as he fingered a squirrel-nibbled cone.
"Back to the year *1835*!! Back to their watery Kingdom beneath the sea...!" smiled the Magician at last.
"We won't be seeing the likes of *them* again!" burst Jamie, throwing his cone into the large patch of grass where *Deer Leap* should have stood.
But then the Magician's smile melted away and a frown replaced it.
"And that is *another* unforgivable error I have made!" he snapped.
"What?" wondered Jamie, throwing another cone and hitting the first.
"I left behind, in the depths of history, a single item I used in one of my disguises! If the Goblins get hold of *that*...!"
But he didn't finish!
The children had sprung to their feet!
Deer Leap was arriving!!

Before their very eyes, the same invisible hands that had built the crystal bridge at Whitby, were constructing their cottage! Slowly but surely, like some kind of three-dimensional painting, the full-sized outside walls were built from the ground upwards, with windows and every detail. Then the roof and the chimney were stuck on! Then the garden with Jessica's animal hutches...the lawn...the fences...the shed!

The small garden wall at the front! The Land-Rover! The stone porch! The front-door! Everything!
Jessica and Jamie rushed forwards to peep through the living-room window! Dad just *had* to be there!
But there wasn't a thing to be seen!
The house was just an empty shell!
Nothing! Not a single room!
The children were crest-fallen and looked over towards Lucius.
But he'd vanished...along with Gabrielle, the chestnut mare!
Just Chandar and Strike were there, gently nibbling the grass.
They looked back through the window...and *this time*!!
Wow!
It was incredible!
Unbelievable!
Everything was there! Exactly as they'd seen the room in the glass box standing next to *The Golphin* under the crystal sea-bed!
Every single piece of furniture...but most importantly...
their father!!
In his favourite armchair!
Munching his *Frosties*!
Gazing at a TV with no picture, just snowy, zig-zag interference!!

Jamie knocked on the window!
Mr Dawson nearly jumped out of his skin.
His head swung round, he glanced at his children and then back at the interference.
It was as if nothing had ever happened!!
"Wasn't expecting you two back so soon! Blinkin' telly's on the blink!" he grumbled, shovelling another spoonful into his mouth. "Just when the program was getting interesting, too! We're going to *have* to get a new one, you know!"

When Jessica crawled into bed that night, her mind was buzzing! A whirl of thoughts and images of the strange adventure spun around her head. She knew she'd never get to sleep!
She tossed and turned! She stared wide-eyed into the darkness!

Buried her head in her pillow!
But still, the pictures wouldn't go away!
First, images of her waking up in that little, crystal room down in *Aqua Crysta*....then the crystalid ride through the Floss Cavern, the beginning of the spectacular show, '*In a Nutshell*'...sitting next to the Queen!
Her heart fell like a stone and tears welled in her eyes.
But then, relentlessly, the pictures kept going on and on... pouring into her head, like a movie!
The journey up the well and over the Moors, the lorry hitting the albino deer, sitting on the quayside eating breakfast, meeting the kids in '*Sherlock's*' cafe, ice-cream on the Abbey Steps, the Count Dracula tour-guide, the underground Victorian street, trapped in the cottage by the Saltw...

...at last, the pictures stopped...
...and she fell into a deep sleep...

But then, in the middle of the night...she awoke!
Her eyes shot open!
The pitch black of her bedroom was frightening!
Where was she?
Pillo or *Deer Leap*?
She closed her eyes and then opened them again.
The darkness was still there!
But something strange was happening!
Something *very strange*!!

A faint glow was coming from near her bedside lamp.
Just beneath it. A peculiar, sort of silvery glow!
The glow began to swell...and illuminate the rest of the room.
She could see her wardrobe, her desk, the curtains, the bookcase...all lit in the silvery glow.
She closed her eyes and immediately opened them.
She gasped and her sleepy eyes widened.
She couldn't believe what she could see!

She was in the tiny, crystal room in *Pillo*!
The giant acorn, the wooden table with the hole, the jay feather sweeping up to the ceiling!
And someone was standing in the doorway!
Someone with a long, green gown, long flowing fair hair and a simple golden coronet!!
Queen Venetia!!
Jessica blinked...and in a trice the image had gone!
She was back in her bedroom at *Deer Leap*!
Still lit by the strange, silvery glow.

And then...she saw it!
By her bedside lamp.
Something was forming!
A shape...out of nothing!

Those invisible fingers again!

Chapter 28

Within seconds, their work was done.
And there lay the most beautiful...
...but surely it couldn't be real...
...Jessica reached out...and cautiously touched it with a finger-tip...

It *was* real!
It *was* there!
A box, like a jewel-box, covered in thousands of fragments of pinky-rosy crystal, lay by her bed. On the lid, picked out in darker, ruby crystals were four letters...
A, C, Q, V...Aqua Crysta, Queen Venetia.
Jessica swung her legs from beneath her duvet and sat on the edge of her bed. Carefully, she reached forward and lifted the small, glistening chest and placed it gently on her lap.
What was its secret?
What did it hold?
In the quiet of the night, lit by the faint, silvery glow...her fingers explored the edges of the lid.
Dare she open it?

She *had* to, she told herself.
The magic had brought it to her!
There must be a reason.
Slowly she raised the hinged lid.
A narrow gap opened on three sides...
...and instantly, a brilliant, intense, white light poured out into the room, flooding over her bed, lapping the floor, the walls, the furniture!
It was so dazzling, so painfully bright, that she wanted to cover her eyes!
She almost closed the box to take away the aching glare...but she knew that she *had* to discover its secret!
Through tightly squinted eyes, she slowly lifted the lid even further!
And the wider and wider the box yawned open, the more the dazzling radiance filled her bedroom. It was as though it had been building up under the lid for years and years, trapped and chained in the chest... and now its brilliance had finally been released! It had escaped and been allowed to bloom!
But strangely, its blossom was short-lived and fleeting.
For, no sooner had it reached its brightest...it faded and vanished!
And the blinding white had dissolved and gone, melted away.

The room fell into its customary night-time darkness and Jessica gazed into the mystical box. It was empty!
Just a faint, silvery glow came from its inside walls...but they appeared glassy, see-through, transparent!
She looked at the outside of the box where the encrusted crystal made the sides solid...but from the inside she could see out! It was most peculiar!
And then...before her eyes...she began to see something forming in the middle of the box, hovering away from the sides...
Slowly it took shape...a creamy, white roll...a roll of parchment, with crinkled, tarnished edges...tied with a scarlet and golden bow!
Jessica reached into the box to gently grasp it...but her fingers fell straight through! She felt nothing!
She drew her hand back and tried again...
Once more the touched emptiness!
There was nothing there...but she could *see* it!

And then, to her astonishment...the bow, by itself, loosened and fell away, vanishing through the glassy base of the box.
Then...magically...the creamy, white parchment began to slowly unroll...again, by itself!
The same entwined letters that were on the lid of the box appeared on the paper, this time in gold and silver.
Next, on the left...delicate, purply, ink-written words came into view as Jessica stared at the unrolling parchment, scarcely believing what was happening before her eyes.

'*To my dear Jessica...*'

The parchment continued to unroll...and then, just as she heard her mother's voice when she opened her Book of Nature, she heard Queen Venetia's voice reading the letter.

As the parchment slowly unrolled, Jessica read the words and listened to them in total and utter amazement!

"To my dear Jessica,

You have been a faithful servant and protector of Our Land.
You are held in the highest esteem by its people.
I, therefore, have the greatest and utmost confidence in the decision and words that follow:-

This is My Last Will as Queen, and is written with the full support and strength of my Chief Advisor, Lepho,
and with the unquestioned loyalty and trust of the people.
Should I fail to return to my Beloved Realm, or die in its cause, then I hereby entrust the Throne and Governance of Aqua Crysta to you,
Jessica.

I wish you well,
and may Good Fortune be always with you,

Venetia"

Then, as the familiar, regal voice faded, the parchment slowly began to roll itself up and the scarlet and golden ribbon re-appeared from nowhere. Silently it wrapped itself around the solemn document and tied the bow.
Jessica, her head spinning from the words, reached once more into the box and touched the parchment.
This time it was *real*!
It was *there*!
Hovering in the silvery glow!
She gently took it from the glassy, crystal box and stared at it, thoughts streaming through her mind.

She just *couldn't* believe it!
She...Jessica...was to be *Queen of Aqua Crysta*!!!

She closed her eyes and shook her head!

This just *had* to be a dream!!

Watch our Website
aquacrysta.com

for the 2010 publication date of

Aqua Crysta - Part 6
'Casket of Shadows'

Follow Jessica and Jamie in yet another thrilling, action-packed adventure set beneath the Forest in the magical, 'reality-meets-fantasy' World of Aqua Crysta!

How can Jessica live at 'Deer Leap' in the real world and be Queen of Aqua Crysta at the same time?

What new, unexpected dangers and challenges suddenly face the young Queen?

Have Jessica and Jamie seen the last of the fearsome Grykes and their Goblin King?

What exactly did the Magician Lucius leave behind in his 1835 Whitby spell?

Look forward to all this and much more in

'Casket of Shadows'
by James David

Part 6 of the 'Aqua Crysta' Series

In a Nutshell!
by Dillip Penlop

'In a Nutshell!'

by Dillip Penlop

Deep, deep, deep, in shady depths of green,
Where crushing footfalls have never been.
Beyond crowds of bustling, thorny tangles,
Stinging nettle and matted brambles.
In depths so deep that no man disturbs,
Where bluebell tinkles can just be heard,
And probing paths cannot lead eyes to see,
Forget-me-nots never to memories plea...

All at once, beneath towering beeches,
Amid the deepest, darkest reaches,
By curly fronds of fern which gently sway,
And lap the toes of walnut trees all day...
There a dappled patch secretly nestles,
Where stems and roots have never wrestled.
A rounded plot of mellow, mottled hues,
Where velvet moss, silky grasses fuse.

So bare a heart of calm confusion,
Yet well castled from all intrusion.
But, if you fought and won and braved the stings,
The scars and scratches, creepy crawly things,
And softly kneel with no rustling bracken,
Not one twig snappin' and crackin'.
Then through the last defences breathless peer,
Within your gaze, strange sights appear!

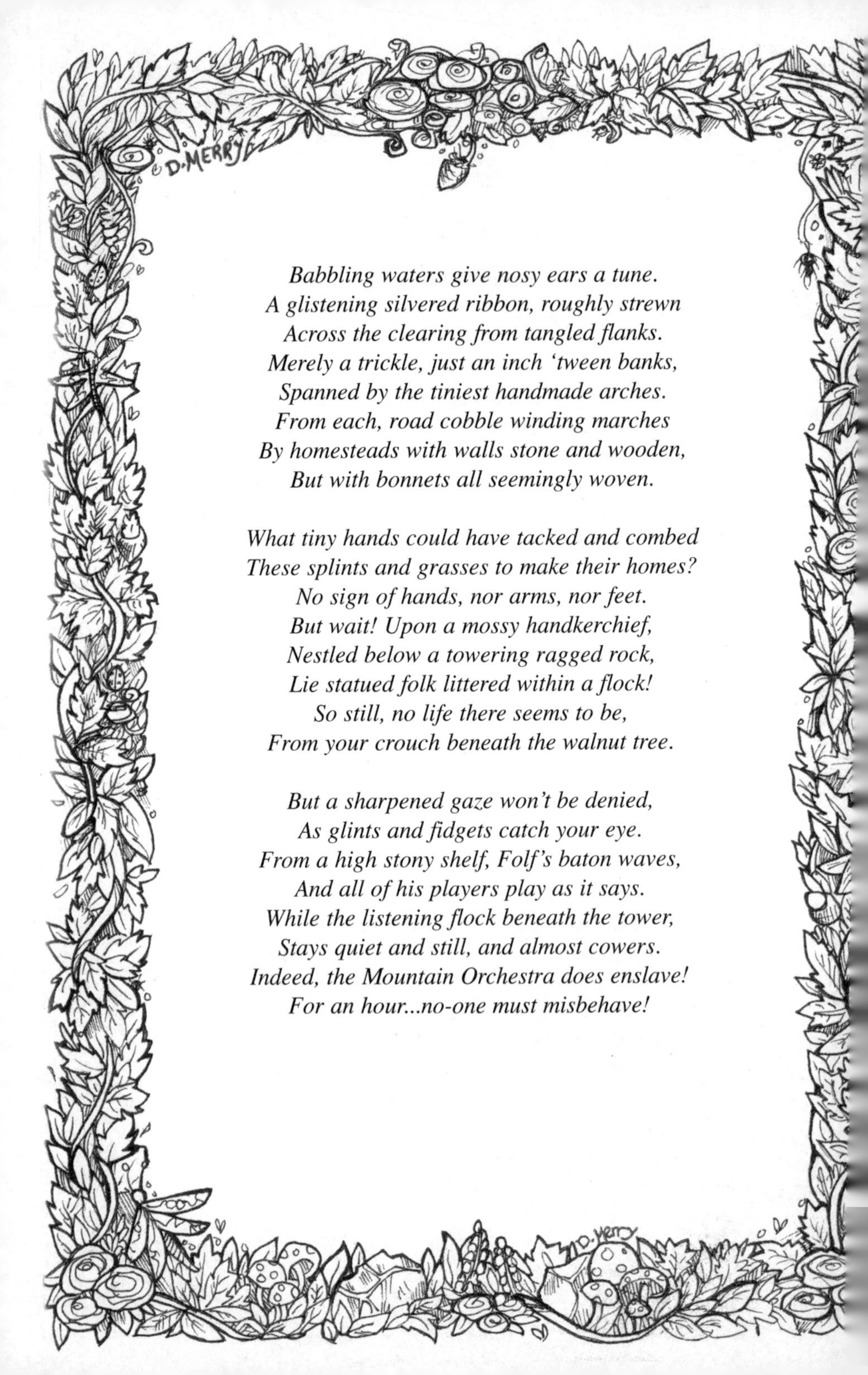

Babbling waters give nosy ears a tune.
A glistening silvered ribbon, roughly strewn
Across the clearing from tangled flanks.
Merely a trickle, just an inch 'tween banks,
Spanned by the tiniest handmade arches.
From each, road cobble winding marches
By homesteads with walls stone and wooden,
But with bonnets all seemingly woven.

What tiny hands could have tacked and combed
These splints and grasses to make their homes?
No sign of hands, nor arms, nor feet.
But wait! Upon a mossy handkerchief,
Nestled below a towering ragged rock,
Lie statued folk littered within a flock!
So still, no life there seems to be,
From your crouch beneath the walnut tree.

But a sharpened gaze won't be denied,
As glints and fidgets catch your eye.
From a high stony shelf, Folf's baton waves,
And all of his players play as it says.
While the listening flock beneath the tower,
Stays quiet and still, and almost cowers.
Indeed, the Mountain Orchestra does enslave!
For an hour...no-one must misbehave!

Any wrongs will be righted by the 'Seat'!
Elders, who on the rocky summit meet.
And from their dizzy perch they sit and stare,
Watching for any soul who risks a dare!
Commands must be followed to the letter,
Or culprits find themselves in chain and fetter!
Laws demand when and how, who does what,
And ordeals are hard for those who've forgot!

When one works and what one makes,
What one wears and how one plays!
Even how to spend the day's 'Free-Hour',
Sat all ears...beneath Folf's Tower!
Original thoughts and deeds do lead to jail,
And this, indeed, sparks off our tale!
Music-making, Dandy Lopp's passion and love,
So entwined, he failed to hear from above...

Folf's Mountain Orchestra strike up its tune,
Marking the onset of 'Free-Hour-at-Noon'!
"Not Dandy again, tuning his violin!"
Broken windows brought not a grin.
All teeth were veiled, though inwardly grinding.
Dandy, again, would need some reminding!
Shouts and demands, "Seat, cart him away!
We want crotchets and quavers without delay!"

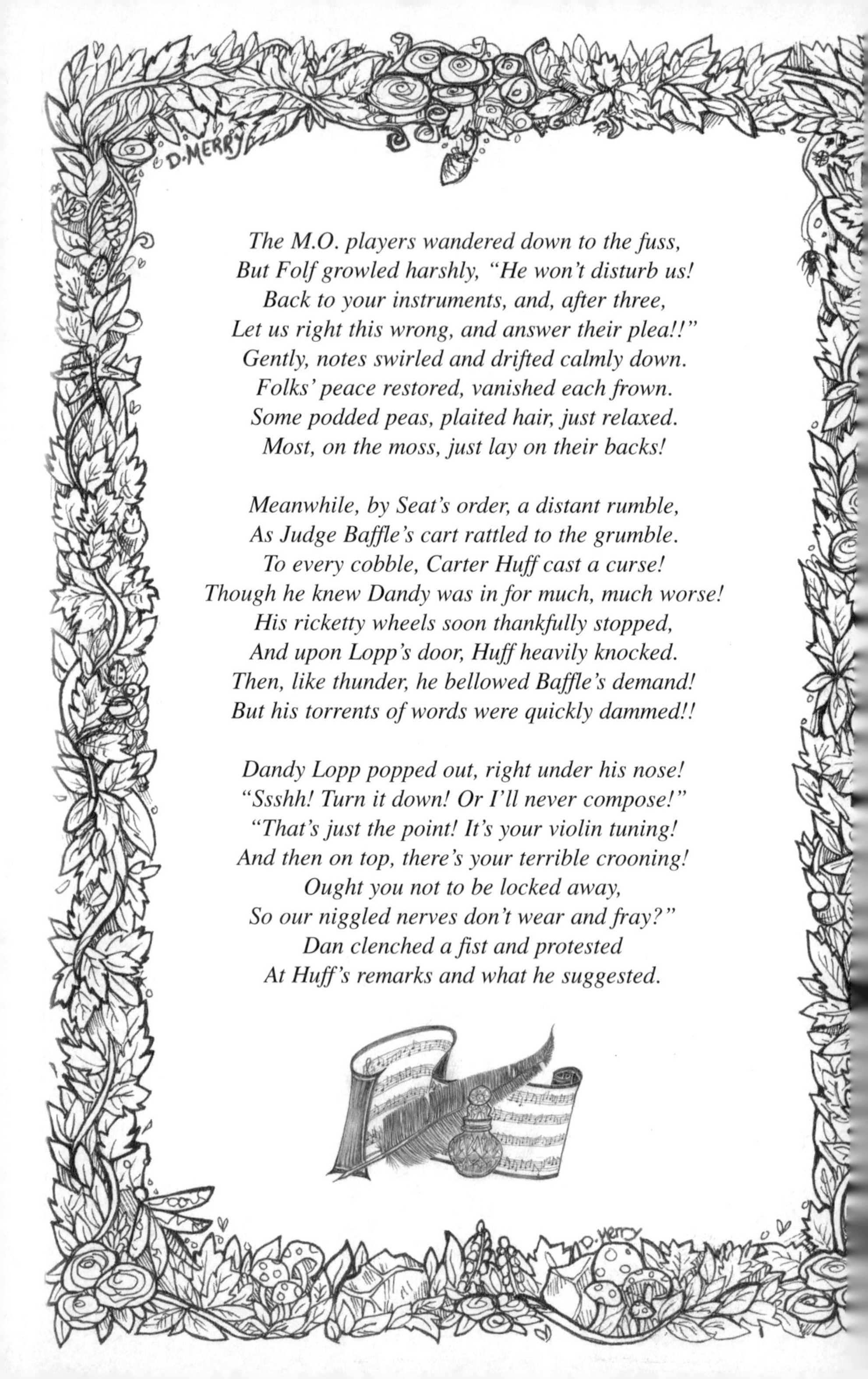

The M.O. players wandered down to the fuss,
But Folf growled harshly, "He won't disturb us!
Back to your instruments, and, after three,
Let us right this wrong, and answer their plea!!"
Gently, notes swirled and drifted calmly down.
Folks' peace restored, vanished each frown.
Some podded peas, plaited hair, just relaxed.
Most, on the moss, just lay on their backs!

Meanwhile, by Seat's order, a distant rumble,
As Judge Baffle's cart rattled to the grumble.
To every cobble, Carter Huff cast a curse!
Though he knew Dandy was in for much, much worse!
His ricketty wheels soon thankfully stopped,
And upon Lopp's door, Huff heavily knocked.
Then, like thunder, he bellowed Baffle's demand!
But his torrents of words were quickly dammed!!

Dandy Lopp popped out, right under his nose!
"Ssshh! Turn it down! Or I'll never compose!"
"That's just the point! It's your violin tuning!
And then on top, there's your terrible crooning!
Ought you not to be locked away,
So our niggled nerves don't wear and fray?"
Dan clenched a fist and protested
At Huff's remarks and what he suggested.

"So, the Seat, once again, wants me in prison!
Come on then, let me hear its decision!"
On the way, Dandy considered the past,
And all the punishment he must have amassed!
For the countless wrongs of his bubbly mind,
With cells and threats, the Seat had tried to bind.
Why was it not, that within his Free-Hour,
He could not let his thoughts just sprout and flower?

But now he was set on the stairs to the Seat,
A spiral of steps that groaned 'neath his feet.
One more creak and he'd reach the summit.
A false step now and he'd surely plummet!
When Dan dared his eyes to glance around,
They traced the road homeward over the ground.
Back to his house and all that he treasured,
Its value to him just couldn't be measured.

Then, all fell quiet, and the Seat settled down,
It now had to sentence this imputant clown!
"Goodbye to your comforts!" Judge Baffle spluttered.
"But 'tis beyond my power!" Loppy muttered.
"My wealth lies snugly under my hat,
Thoughts are my riches, can't deny that!
In a cell lock me, with no interruptions,
And my mind will blossom in mighty eruptions!"

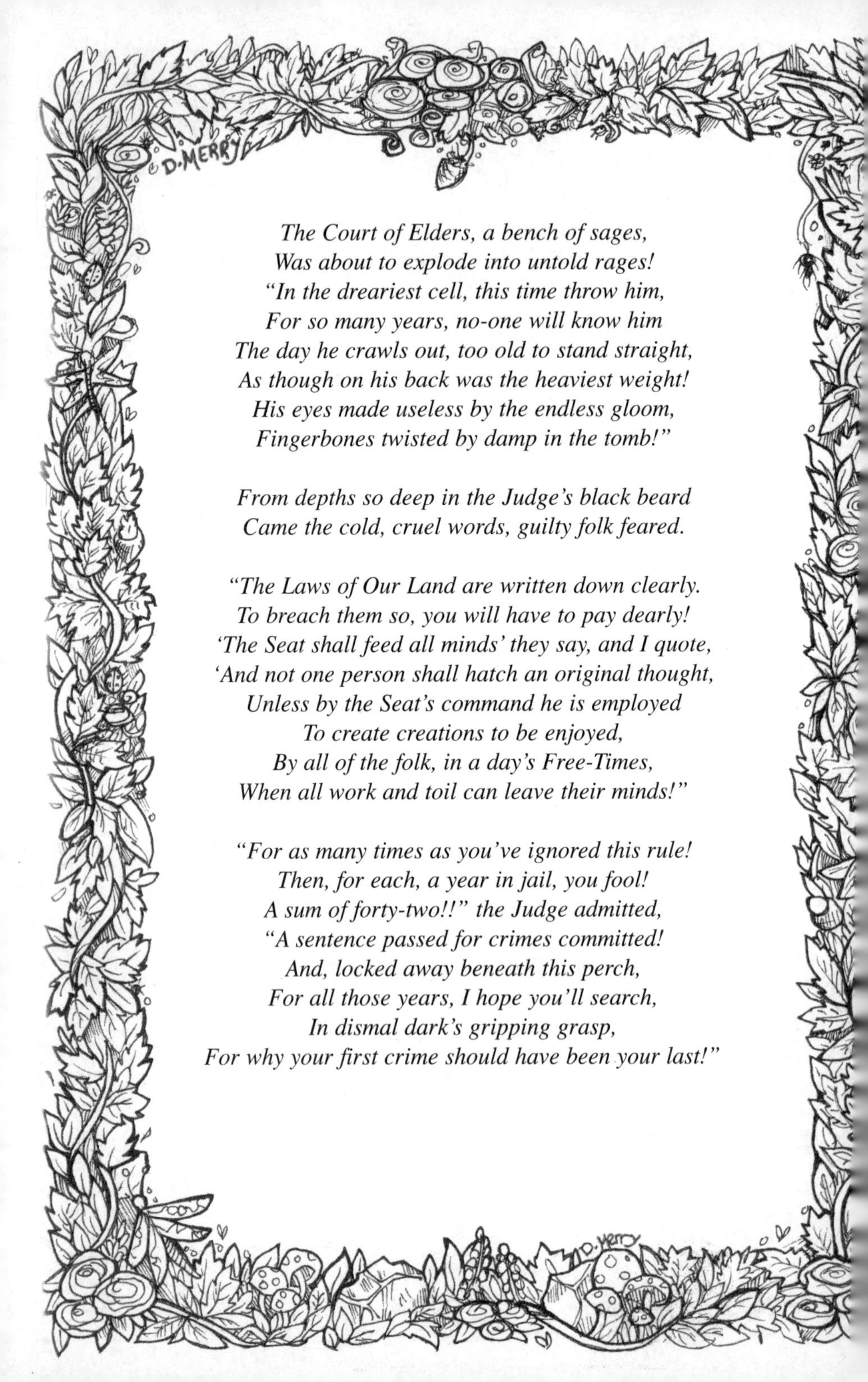

The Court of Elders, a bench of sages,
Was about to explode into untold rages!
"In the dreariest cell, this time throw him,
For so many years, no-one will know him
The day he crawls out, too old to stand straight,
As though on his back was the heaviest weight!
His eyes made useless by the endless gloom,
Fingerbones twisted by damp in the tomb!"

From depths so deep in the Judge's black beard
Came the cold, cruel words, guilty folk feared.

"The Laws of Our Land are written down clearly.
To breach them so, you will have to pay dearly!
'The Seat shall feed all minds' they say, and I quote,
'And not one person shall hatch an original thought,
Unless by the Seat's command he is employed
To create creations to be enjoyed,
By all of the folk, in a day's Free-Times,
When all work and toil can leave their minds!"

"For as many times as you've ignored this rule!
Then, for each, a year in jail, you fool!
A sum of forty-two!!" the Judge admitted,
"A sentence passed for crimes committed!
And, locked away beneath this perch,
For all those years, I hope you'll search,
In dismal dark's gripping grasp,
For why your first crime should have been your last!"

Dandy sank upon the floor and sadly sighed.
With head bowed low, tears flood his eyes.
Then dragged away without a sound,
To a lofty shelf far off the ground.
The Seat sat, gazed and smugly peered,
While below, the orchestra loudly cheered.
With a grinding groan, the cell jaws clench.
In darkness, Dan stumbles to a rough cut bench.

"Nookish crannies, candles and spills,
For well fed pantries, inks and quills!"
Whispers Dandy to himself in solemn tones,
Of pity and sadness through to his bones.
Perched on a bench amid a walnut shell,
Jagged walls and roof make up his cell.
The jaws don't close, a gap just gleams.
Never dazzling daylight, just hopeful beams.

Never gales but draughts, never floods but drips,
A flickering candle for company he grips.
The flame grows long, squats, weaves a spell,
Then upward stabs and crowns the swell,
With a slender, weaving, smoky plume,
As bold shadows beckon across the gloom.
And his wretched eyes sadly give in,
Having shown Dandy the world he now lives in.

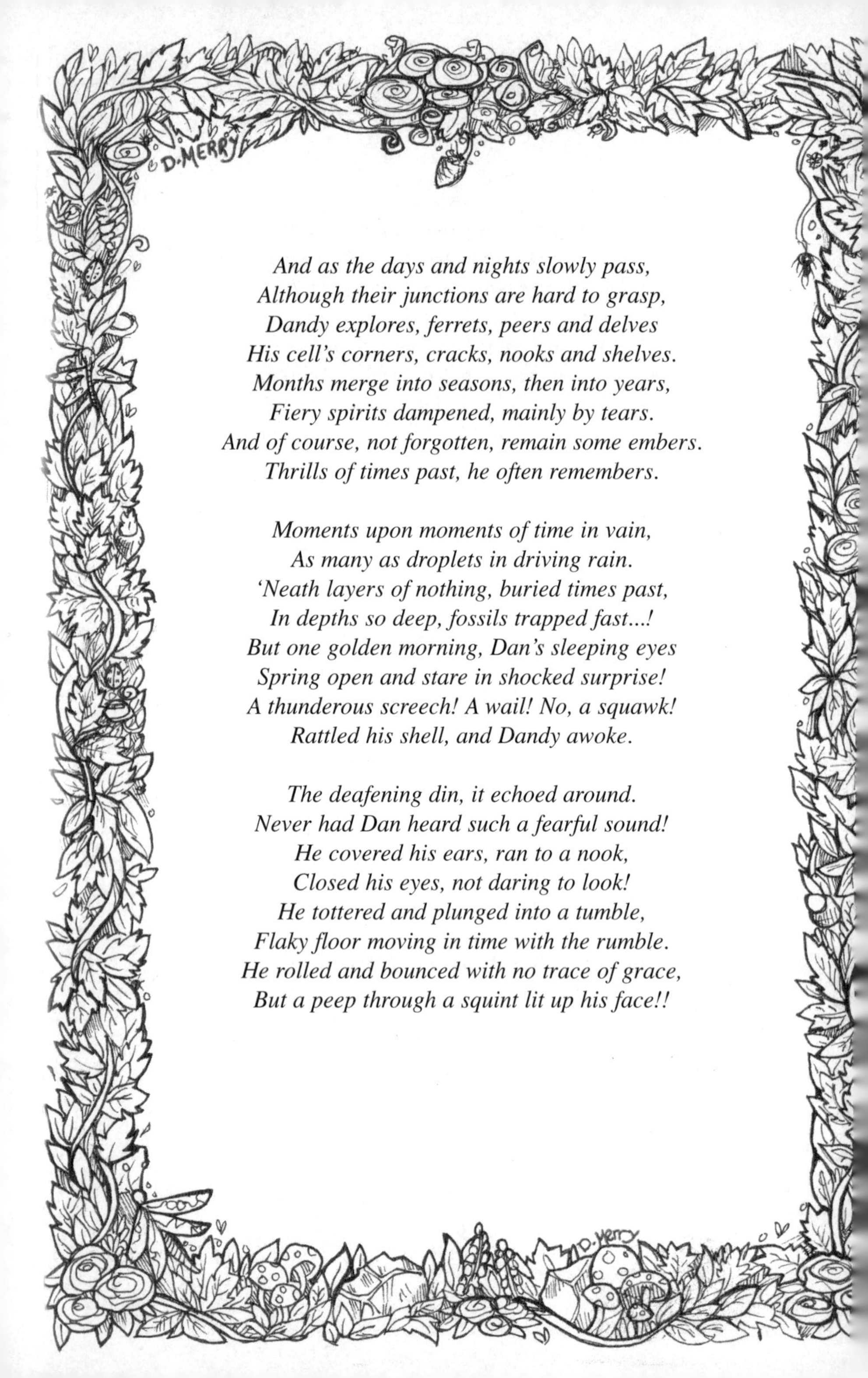

And as the days and nights slowly pass,
Although their junctions are hard to grasp,
Dandy explores, ferrets, peers and delves
His cell's corners, cracks, nooks and shelves.
Months merge into seasons, then into years,
Fiery spirits dampened, mainly by tears.
And of course, not forgotten, remain some embers.
Thrills of times past, he often remembers.

Moments upon moments of time in vain,
As many as droplets in driving rain.
'Neath layers of nothing, buried times past,
In depths so deep, fossils trapped fast...!
But one golden morning, Dan's sleeping eyes
Spring open and stare in shocked surprise!
A thunderous screech! A wail! No, a squawk!
Rattled his shell, and Dandy awoke.

The deafening din, it echoed around.
Never had Dan heard such a fearful sound!
He covered his ears, ran to a nook,
Closed his eyes, not daring to look!
He tottered and plunged into a tumble,
Flaky floor moving in time with the rumble.
He rolled and bounced with no trace of grace,
But a peep through a squint lit up his face!!

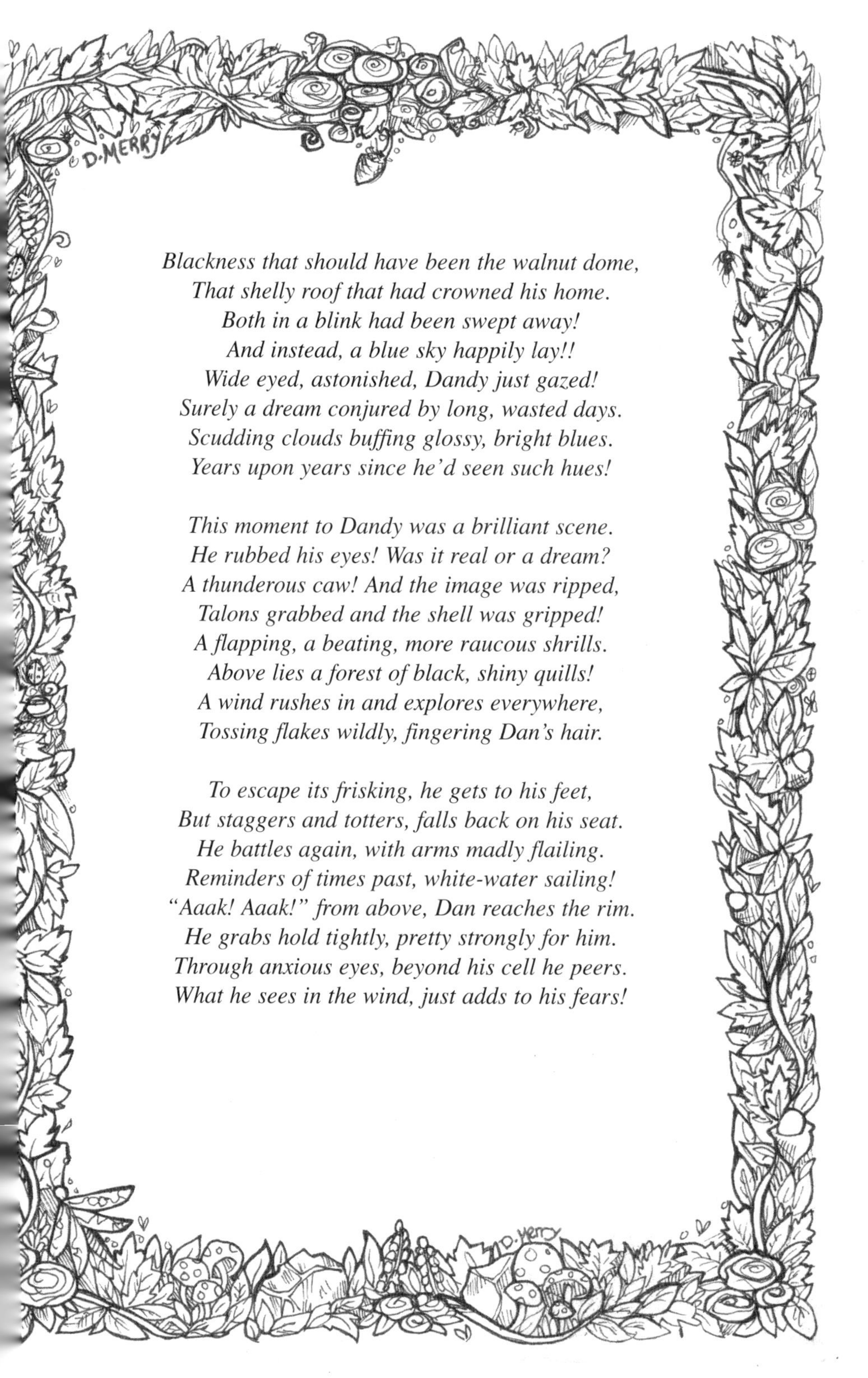

Blackness that should have been the walnut dome,
That shelly roof that had crowned his home.
Both in a blink had been swept away!
And instead, a blue sky happily lay!!
Wide eyed, astonished, Dandy just gazed!
Surely a dream conjured by long, wasted days.
Scudding clouds buffing glossy, bright blues.
Years upon years since he'd seen such hues!

This moment to Dandy was a brilliant scene.
He rubbed his eyes! Was it real or a dream?
A thunderous caw! And the image was ripped,
Talons grabbed and the shell was gripped!
A flapping, a beating, more raucous shrills.
Above lies a forest of black, shiny quills!
A wind rushes in and explores everywhere,
Tossing flakes wildly, fingering Dan's hair.

To escape its frisking, he gets to his feet,
But staggers and totters, falls back on his seat.
He battles again, with arms madly flailing.
Reminders of times past, white-water sailing!
"Aaak! Aaak!" from above, Dan reaches the rim.
He grabs hold tightly, pretty strongly for him.
Through anxious eyes, beyond his cell he peers.
What he sees in the wind, just adds to his fears!

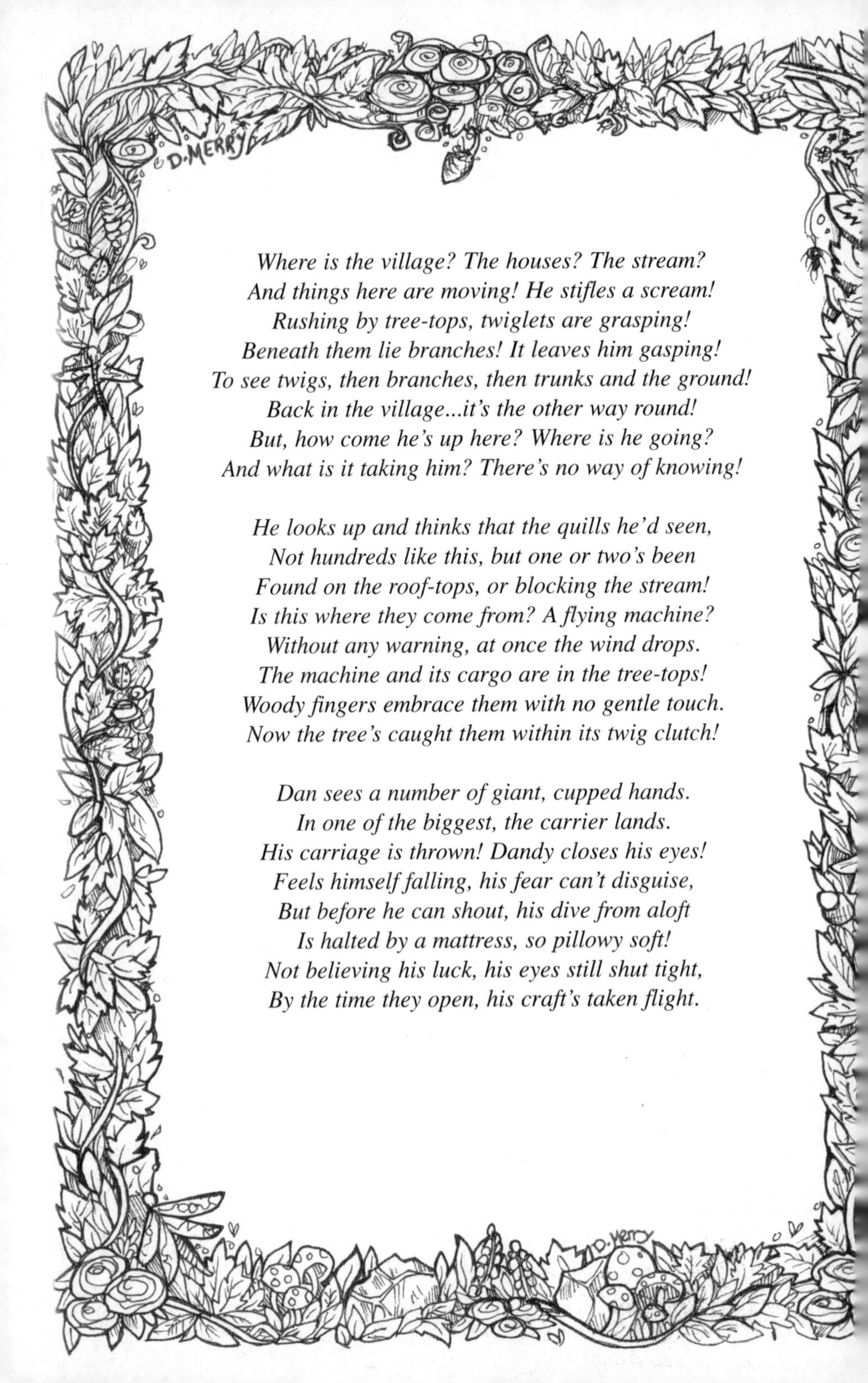

Where is the village? The houses? The stream?
And things here are moving! He stifles a scream!
Rushing by tree-tops, twiglets are grasping!
Beneath them lie branches! It leaves him gasping!
To see twigs, then branches, then trunks and the ground!
Back in the village...it's the other way round!
But, how come he's up here? Where is he going?
And what is it taking him? There's no way of knowing!

He looks up and thinks that the quills he'd seen,
Not hundreds like this, but one or two's been
Found on the roof-tops, or blocking the stream!
Is this where they come from? A flying machine?
Without any warning, at once the wind drops.
The machine and its cargo are in the tree-tops!
Woody fingers embrace them with no gentle touch.
Now the tree's caught them within its twig clutch!

Dan sees a number of giant, cupped hands.
In one of the biggest, the carrier lands.
His carriage is thrown! Dandy closes his eyes!
Feels himself falling, his fear can't disguise,
But before he can shout, his dive from aloft
Is halted by a mattress, so pillowy soft!
Not believing his luck, his eyes still shut tight,
By the time they open, his craft's taken flight.

The sight beyond twiglets is so deep and so wide,
A view, until now, Dan's been totally denied!
Although these scenes have formed in his mind,
Towards them his friends were always unkind.
All through his life, Dan knew there was more,
Lying quietly in wait, a world to explore.
But unbending, unyielding, were the Seat's harsh rules.
Dandy convinced they were thought of by fools!

Just then, a sharp crack pierced his ears.
At once, the wondrous landscape flooded by fears.
He turned to see even more strange sights!
Shapes so peculiar...and to such towering heights!
So white and so smooth, so hard and so round!
Nothing quite like them grew on the ground!
Their beautiful form was a feast for the eyes,
But their sudden explosion had been a surprise!

They appeared unmoving, so calm and serene,
Not prone to disturbance upsetting the scene.
As he stared up in awe, one split loudly asunder,
From tip to toe, a crack amid thunder!
Shattered shell fragments fell from the shape,
As a bony, yellow point stabbed through the gape.
Hatching in Lopp, new seeds of fearful doubt.
He had to look smart for a rapid way out!!

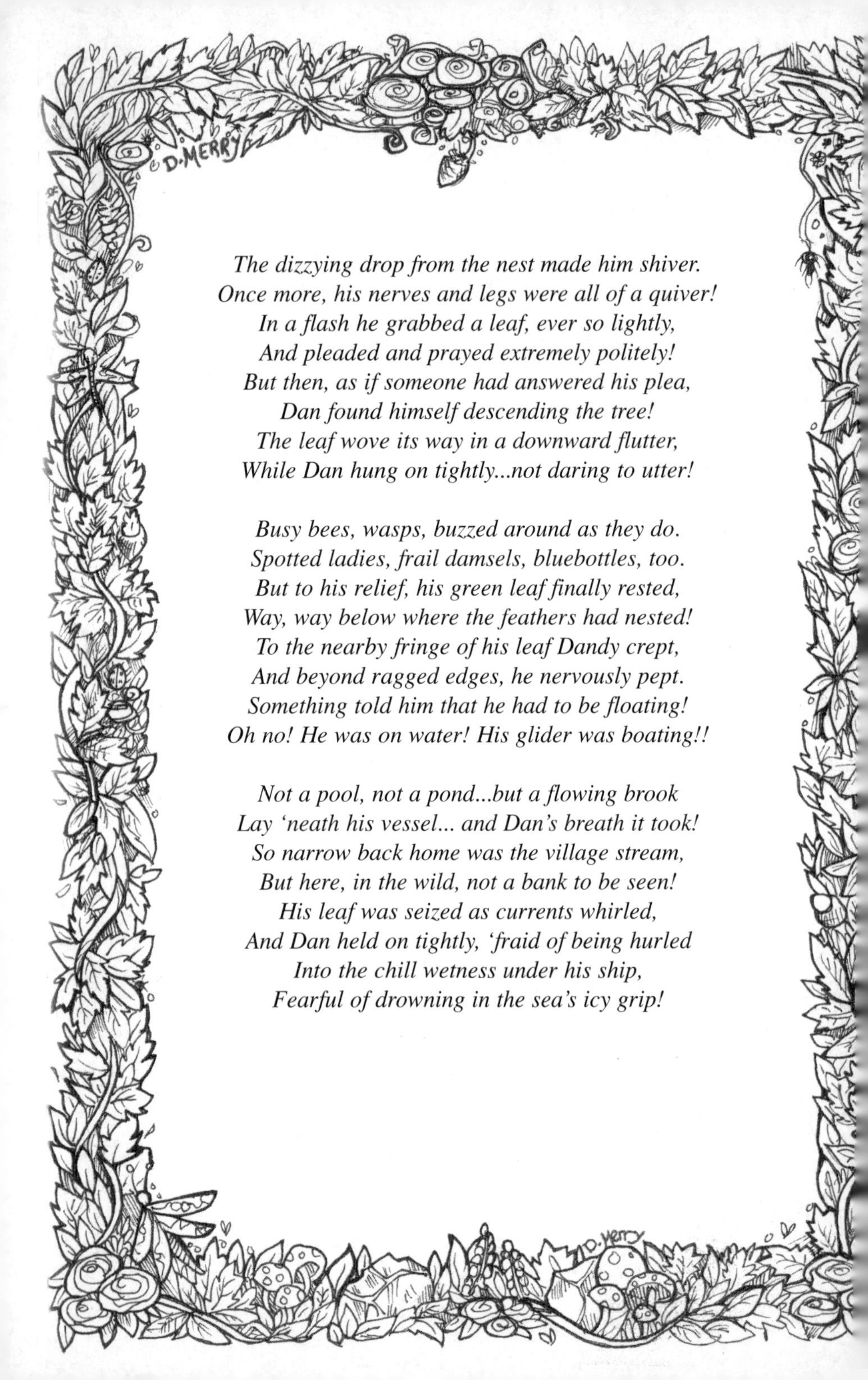

The dizzying drop from the nest made him shiver.
Once more, his nerves and legs were all of a quiver!
In a flash he grabbed a leaf, ever so lightly,
And pleaded and prayed extremely politely!
But then, as if someone had answered his plea,
Dan found himself descending the tree!
The leaf wove its way in a downward flutter,
While Dan hung on tightly...not daring to utter!

Busy bees, wasps, buzzed around as they do.
Spotted ladies, frail damsels, bluebottles, too.
But to his relief, his green leaf finally rested,
Way, way below where the feathers had nested!
To the nearby fringe of his leaf Dandy crept,
And beyond ragged edges, he nervously pept.
Something told him that he had to be floating!
Oh no! He was on water! His glider was boating!!

Not a pool, not a pond...but a flowing brook
Lay 'neath his vessel... and Dan's breath it took!
So narrow back home was the village stream,
But here, in the wild, not a bank to be seen!
His leaf was seized as currents whirled,
And Dan held on tightly, 'fraid of being hurled
Into the chill wetness under his ship,
Fearful of drowning in the sea's icy grip!

'Tween roots and rocks he wound and he wove,
Wishing he'd wash up in a calm, quiet cove.
Onward and onward the wild water sped him,
Goodness only knows where he was heading!
But as the raging river rounded a bend
Dandy caught sight of his long journey's end.
For there under boughs to give him some shade,
Was a spot that was for him, ideally made!

His leaf rode the ripples and gently landed
On a safe, sloping shore, smooth and sanded.
Panting and gasping, his clothes soggy drenched,
From his ride on a nightmare, at last he was wrenched!
Face down in the sand, he rested and slept,
For safety, one eye open, he sensibly kept.
Where had he come to, from his walnut shell?
How many days walk, it was hard to tell!

But he knew in his dreams he would never return,
To have the Seat's lessons again to re-learn!
Instead he would live on this foreign shore,
Build a house with windows, a roof and a door.
Like a wrecked soul cast on a lonely isle,
He vowed to survive for many a while.
Whatever he did, it was certainly better
Than locked in a cell, under chain and fetter!

Now, creations could blossom, they could bloom,
Never again to be trapped in that tomb.
Time flew by, from days into weeks.
Life had its lows as well as its peaks.
But from each day's dawn, 'til when it was dark,
Even night through, 'til owl hears the lark,
Dan kept himself busy and built a snug house,
And lined it with moss and fur from a mouse.

He thatched it with bracken and splinters of wood,
All firmed and fast with handfuls of mud.
Inside he bound twiglets with threads of coarse grass,
And tables and chairs, they began to amass.
With simple tools he carved a musical flute,
And then came a drum, and even a lute!
Along with the robins, finches and thrushes,
Music he made, at last with no hushes!

Here at last, a place to play and compose,
Contented from finger-tips down to his toes.
Inks made from juices, and pine-needle pens.
In no time at all, he'd made some good friends,
Though he'd eyed not one person, not one single soul,
His company was splendid...except for a mole!
For it insisted, it seemed, on building a hill,
In Dandy's garden, for some kind of thrill!

The mountain reached higher, and soon blocked the light,
It was, to Dan's eyes, a terrible sight!
But a yearning came over him, one starry night,
As a break in the story he'd started to write,
To go for a walk, a stroll 'neath the moon,
Just for a breather, he'd be back soon.
With his stick in his hand, he made for the heap,
Perhaps he would climb it...just for a peep!

There he could see what the forest may hide,
Way beyond secrets, on the other side.
Half-way he had climbed when his legs said, 'Enough!'
They'd not thought of strolling as being this tough!
He sat in the moonshine and gazed down the slope,
Legs willing bedwards, and aching in hope.
Below him, in silver, his beautiful home!
A sight worth seeing from the top of the dome!!

Limbs staggered onwards to the tip of the peak,
When they'd made it, they were ever so weak!
But the views from the summit were worthy of toil,
A marvel of magic, this mountain of soil!
His house looked so small, by the wide water stretch,
The next time he came, a chair he would fetch!
Though when he turned round and stared far ahead,
What he saw twinkling...filled him with dread!!

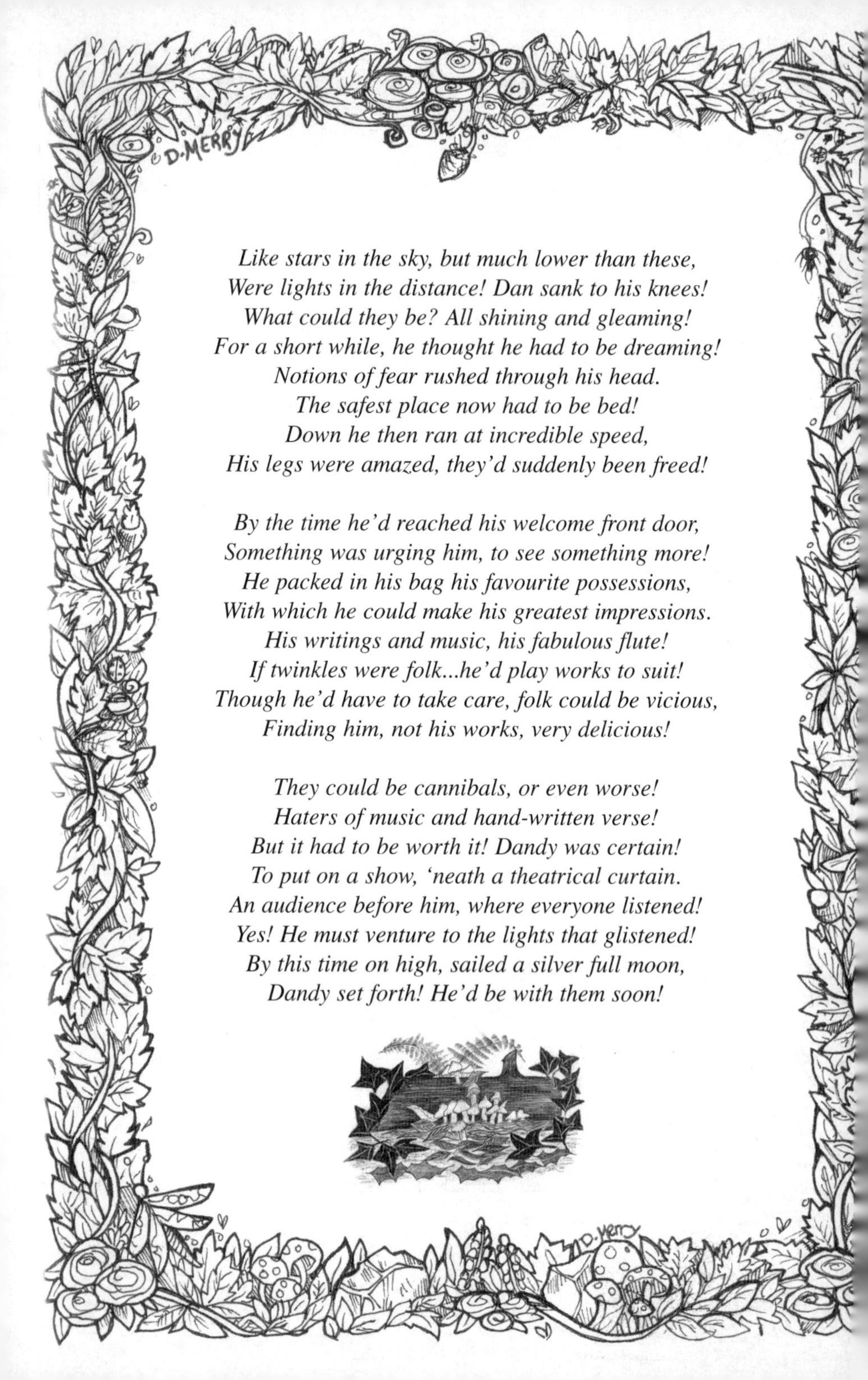

Like stars in the sky, but much lower than these,
Were lights in the distance! Dan sank to his knees!
What could they be? All shining and gleaming!
For a short while, he thought he had to be dreaming!
Notions of fear rushed through his head.
The safest place now had to be bed!
Down he then ran at incredible speed,
His legs were amazed, they'd suddenly been freed!

By the time he'd reached his welcome front door,
Something was urging him, to see something more!
He packed in his bag his favourite possessions,
With which he could make his greatest impressions.
His writings and music, his fabulous flute!
If twinkles were folk...he'd play works to suit!
Though he'd have to take care, folk could be vicious,
Finding him, not his works, very delicious!

They could be cannibals, or even worse!
Haters of music and hand-written verse!
But it had to be worth it! Dandy was certain!
To put on a show, 'neath a theatrical curtain.
An audience before him, where everyone listened!
Yes! He must venture to the lights that glistened!
By this time on high, sailed a silver full moon,
Dandy set forth! He'd be with them soon!

By thrift and by thistles, cowslips and clover,
By coltsfoot and bluebells, tramped the brave rover.
Round puddles and pebbles, rambling tree roots,
His bones soon ached, straight down to his boots.
But merry lights twinkling, numbed him to all,
As they drew closer with every footfall.
His pack grew heavy...made it tricky to breathe.
By the wayside, its weight, he wished he could leave!

But its burden, he knew, was the value of gold,
Worthy of hardships, for crowds to behold!
His dream of applause and unbridled cheering
Almost drowned out the owls he was hearing.
So eager, in fact, to succeed and not fail,
He managed to pass a wandering snail!
Which to you, may sound incredibly slow,
But remember, Dan's pace is amazingly low!

But on and on...and the lights they grew bigger,
As bravely onward, sped our venturesome figure!
And then...at last...beneath the setting moon,
The shapes of houses started to loom!
Not little homes, topped with thatched grasses,
But high ones, of tree stumps, clumped into masses!
A city so large, its lights lit his face,
As he nervously pept from a well hidden place.

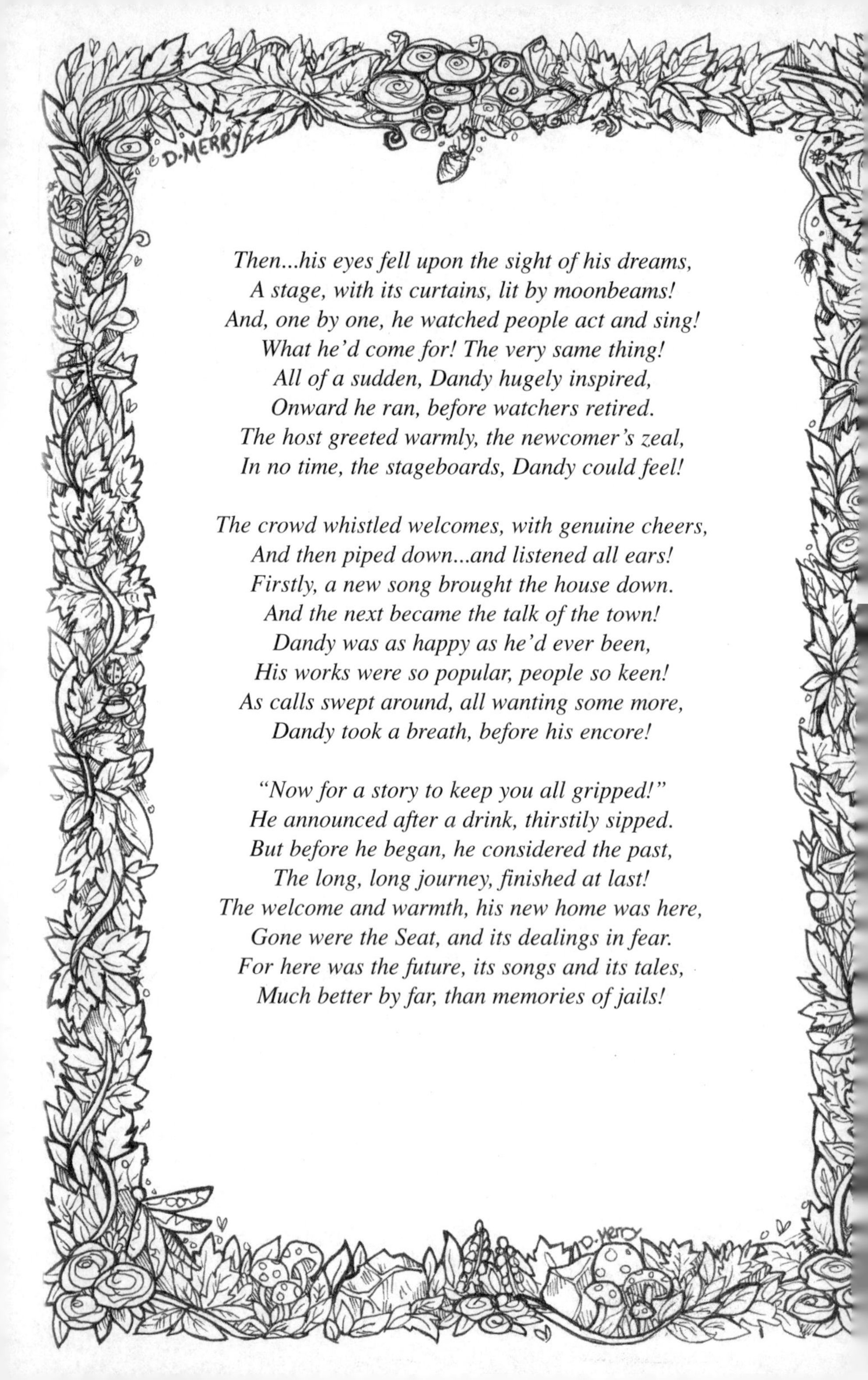

Then...his eyes fell upon the sight of his dreams,
A stage, with its curtains, lit by moonbeams!
And, one by one, he watched people act and sing!
What he'd come for! The very same thing!
All of a sudden, Dandy hugely inspired,
Onward he ran, before watchers retired.
The host greeted warmly, the newcomer's zeal,
In no time, the stageboards, Dandy could feel!

The crowd whistled welcomes, with genuine cheers,
And then piped down...and listened all ears!
Firstly, a new song brought the house down.
And the next became the talk of the town!
Dandy was as happy as he'd ever been,
His works were so popular, people so keen!
As calls swept around, all wanting some more,
Dandy took a breath, before his encore!

"Now for a story to keep you all gripped!"
He announced after a drink, thirstily sipped.
But before he began, he considered the past,
The long, long journey, finished at last!
The welcome and warmth, his new home was here,
Gone were the Seat, and its dealings in fear.
For here was the future, its songs and its tales,
Much better by far, than memories of jails!

Upstepped our Hero, to a frenzied cheering
A new composition, they'd soon all be hearing.
Then, in a voice, as sound as a bell,
This tale of freedom, he needed to tell.
The crowd fell silent, and he began to recite
A tale of imprisonment and fearful flight...

"Deep, deep, deep, in shady depths of green,
Where crushing footfalls have never been..."

At 3 o'clock in the middle of the night,
a mysterious green glow beckons Tom
from his bedroom!
He makes a fantastic, magical discovery
and his life will never be the same again!

Join Tom on his amazing adventures
with his brilliant new secret power!!